On the ocean, no one can hear you scream. . . .

"Get away from the radio, Jessica," Eric warned. His voice was deep and deadly serious.

"Nick! Help!" she continued on, feeling Eric's smoldering eyes burning into the back of her head. Her fingers squeezed the radio mouthpiece desperately. "Help! This is an emergency!"

Eric stood in front of her, the veins in his forearms bulging. "I told you to get away from there," he seethed, but Jessica wouldn't let go. The radio was her only hope.

"Nick!"

"The radio won't help you, Jessica." With prying fingers Eric opened the side compartment and reached into the radio, pulling out a fistful of broken wires. A triumphant grin broke across his face, revealing viciously gleaming white teeth.

Jessica backed away, eyes bulging in terror, hands gripping her head. "Nick! Help me!" she screamed with such ferocity that it felt as if her lungs were on fire. *"Nick!"* But she knew with terrifying dread it was all for nothing. And when she looked out over the water, there was still no sign that Nick was on his way back.

Eric leaned casually against the mast, his grin melting into a flirtatious pout. "Don't bother screaming, sweetheart," he whispered, his stony black eyes leering at her through thick eyelashes. "No one can hear you."

Bantam Books in the Sweet Valley University series.
Ask your bookseller for the books you have missed.

And don't miss these Sweet Valley
University Thriller Editions:

Visit the Official Sweet Valley Web Site on the Internet at:

http://www.sweetvalley.com

SWEET VALLEY UNIVERSITY®

THRILLER EDITION

Killer at Sea

Written by
Laurie John

Created by
FRANCINE PASCAL

BANTAM BOOKS
NEW YORK · TORONTO · LONDON · SYDNEY · AUCKLAND

To Samuel Brashares Collins

RL 6, age 12 and up

KILLER AT SEA

A Bantam Book / July 1997

Sweet Valley High® *and Sweet Valley University*®
are registered trademarks of Francine Pascal.
Conceived by Francine Pascal.
Produced by Daniel Weiss Associates, Inc.
33 West 17th Street
New York, NY 10011.

ISBN: 0-553-57061-7

Published simultaneously in the United States and Canada

Bantam Books are published by Bantam Books, a division of Bantam
Doubleday Dell Publishing Group, Inc. Its trademark, consisting of the
words "Bantam Books" and the portrayal of a rooster, is Registered in
U.S. Patent and Trademark Office and in other countries. Marca
Registrada. Bantam Books, 1540 Broadway, New York, New York 10036.

PRINTED IN THE UNITED STATES OF AMERICA

OPM   0 9 8 7 6 5 4 3 2 1

Chapter
One

"Can you be ready in twenty minutes?" Nick Fox's voice sounded strained and anxious on the other end of the telephone line. "I need to get out of here fast—before I lose my mind."

Jessica Wakefield gave the receiver cord a hurried yank and dragged the phone across the floor of the dorm room to her closet, the door perpetually jammed open by a twisted heap of clothes and shoes. "Let me just throw a few things in my bag. . . ." Jessica's voice trailed off as she dove into the messy pile, frantically searching for her favorite red bikini. Little goose bumps ran excitedly up and down the back of Jessica's neck at the prospect of spontaneous adventure with her boyfriend, Nick. To Jessica, it seemed like years since they had done anything fun together.

"And don't worry about getting a ride," Jessica continued as she eyed a patch of red material that was trapped beneath a pair of high–heeled leather boots in the back of her closet. "Liz will drive us to the marina." With a mental cheer she snatched up her bikini and stuffed it in the nearest bag.

"I'm driving who where?" murmured a softly exasperated voice behind her.

Jessica turned around to see that her twin sister, Elizabeth, had actually come up for air from the thick volume she was reading. The cover was gray and boring and read Ethics in Journalism in big black letters. Elizabeth shook her head slightly, her blue–green eyes narrowing suspiciously.

Jessica raised her brows pleadingly and cradled the receiver between her jaw and shoulder so she could press her palms together in a praying gesture. "Please?" she mouthed silently.

Elizabeth rolled her eyes and turned her attention back to her humongous book.

"Pack light, Jess," Nick warned. "There isn't going to be enough room in the cabin for your entire wardrobe."

"Sure, whatever." Jessica swept her arm across the top of her bureau and her entire makeup collection cascaded like a waterfall into an open backpack below. She packed the over-flow of nail polish bottles into another small cosmetic bag.

Nick sighed loudly as if he could see exactly what she was doing. "I mean it, Jess. It's going to be just you and me and the ocean—all you need is a swimsuit, T-shirts and shorts, and some warm clothes for the evening. Now is *not* the time to be high maintenance."

"OK, fine," Jessica murmured absentmind-edly, looking under her bed for anything impor-tant she might have missed.

"I know exactly what you're doing," Nick insisted, "and I'm begging you to stop. The last things you need for this trip are fourteen shades of nail polish and a pair of high heels."

Speaking of which, where are *my spike heels?* she asked herself, momentarily considering thanking Nick for the unintentional reminder. Shoving aside a box of hair curlers and several dust balls, Jessica was suddenly seized with a gnawing panic. Her sexiest pair of shoes were absolutely nowhere in sight.

"A good pair of sweats is all you really need at night," Nick persisted. "It gets pretty cold and windy out on the water."

Jessica searched behind her desk. Still no shoes. "Look, Nick," she said briskly, a thin film of perspiration beading her forehead. "I'm having a bit of a crisis right now. . . . I'll see you in twenty minutes. OK?"

"Just get here as soon as you can," Nick answered.

As soon as Jessica hung up the phone Elizabeth pounced on her. "What exactly did you volunteer me for *this* time?" Her voice dripped with annoyance.

"Can't talk about this right now, Liz. . . ." Jessica waved her sister away as if she were a pesky fly. "Have you seen my spikes?"

"They're right where you left them." Elizabeth toyed with the end of her neat blond braid. "One is sitting on top of the CD player and the other is in the bottom drawer of your desk."

"Oooh, thanks!" Finding the heels exactly where Elizabeth said they were, Jessica smiled brightly. "You're a genius, Liz. What would I do without you?"

Elizabeth sighed heavily and snapped her book shut. "So now can you tell me what's going on? I have a class in less than an hour."

"It's so cool, Liz!" Jessica squealed, jumping up and down ecstatically. "Nick and I are going on vacation!"

"Vacation?" Elizabeth raised one eyebrow. "Starting right now?"

4

Jessica nodded. "For a whole week. We're renting a yacht!"

Elizabeth stared at her twin blankly. "We're in the middle of the semester, Jess. You can't just take off when you feel like it."

Jessica rolled her eyes as she shoved a mound of clothes into a large suitcase. "It's not like I have a choice or anything. Nick already booked the charter. We leave in an hour."

Elizabeth pursed her lips thoughtfully. "That's strange . . . I thought Nick was busy working on the Horstmueller kidnapping case. Did they finally catch the kidnapper? I didn't see anything about it in the paper this morning."

Jessica shrugged. "I didn't ask any questions—and to be honest, I really don't care. Nick's been so wrapped up in this case for the last few weeks that we've hardly spent any time together, and when we *are* together, his mind is totally somewhere else. This vacation is exactly what he needs to get his priorities straight again."

"And that would be . . . what, exactly?"

"To give me all the attention I deserve, of course," Jessica said matter-of-factly, giving her long blond hair a flip.

"Poor guy," Elizabeth teased. "By the time you're through with him, he's going to wish he was back at work."

Ignoring the comment, Jessica reached for the set of keys hanging on a hook by the front door and tossed them to her sister. "Go bring the Jeep around, would you, pretty please? We have to pick Nick up at the station in ten minutes."

Elizabeth cast a disapproving look at the enormous pile of luggage sitting in the middle of the floor. "The boat is going to sink with all that stuff."

A dreamy look washed over Jessica's face as she closed the last suitcase with a decisive snap. "Joke all you want, Liz, but this is going to be the most incredible, romantic, wonderful vacation Nick and I have ever had!"

"Nick!" Jessica called from the Jeep as she and her sister pulled up to the police precinct. Before Elizabeth even had a chance to bring the vehicle to a full stop, Jessica had already opened the passenger-side door and was hopping out.

Elizabeth puffed an exasperated breath skyward, blowing aside the golden blond wisps that framed her pretty face. *Life with Jessica can be so draining sometimes,* she mused silently, watching her sister throw her arms around Nick on the stone steps of the police station. It was beyond Elizabeth's comprehension how Jessica could just take off on a moment's notice without even giving it a second thought. Midterms were only a week away, but it never even occurred to Jessica that she wouldn't have any time to study for them. Naturally Elizabeth found herself doing all the worrying, trying to think of all the details her sister would invariably forget. Even though she was older by only four minutes, to Elizabeth it sometimes felt more like forty years.

Jessica skipped down the steps in her spike heels and a short baby blue mini paired with a revealing white halter top. While the outfit made the most of her golden California tan, it was the worst possible thing Jessica could wear for an afternoon on the high seas. One small trip in those slippery shoes and she'd be overboard in seconds, or at least stuck floating on a boat in the middle of nowhere with several broken bones.

Don't even worry about it, Elizabeth's inner voice soothed. *She'll figure it out on her own soon enough.* But somehow she figured that wasn't going to be the case.

Nick opened the door and glanced briefly at Elizabeth. Instead of greeting her with his usual friendly smile, Nick's square jaw and finely structured cheekbones were racked with tension. There was a skittish, almost wild look in his deep green eyes that Elizabeth had never seen before. Something was definitely bugging him.

"Hey, Elizabeth," Nick said, keeping his eyes averted from hers. His voice was flat and emotionless.

Elizabeth smiled faintly, her brow knotting with concern. "Hi, N—"

"What is all this junk?" Nick interrupted tensely as he glared at the back of the Jeep.

The muscles in Elizabeth's shoulders seized up when she heard the harshness of Nick's voice. He was usually such a nice, easygoing guy despite his high-pressure job as an undercover cop. What was wrong?

"They're my bags," Jessica said breezily, as if she didn't even sense that her boyfriend was in a rotten mood.

"I told you to pack light," Nick said through gritted teeth.

"I *did*."

"No, you didn't," he barked. "There's hardly any room for me to sit in the backseat!"

Elizabeth groaned inwardly, silently hating how she was dragged away from a peaceful afternoon of reading to listen to Jessica and Nick's bickering. She looked at her watch. At this rate there was no hope of making it to class, let alone the end of the thirty-fourth chapter of *Ethics in Journalism*.

"If something's in your way, then move it."

8

Jessica pointed to one of her enormous cosmetic cases.

"That's not the point," Nick argued. "There isn't enough room on the boat for you to take all your junk. See what I brought?" He held up a single duffel bag as if they were playing show-and-tell. "I have only what I *need*. Bare bones. Nothing fancy."

"I brought what I need too." Jessica crossed her arms stubbornly. "You men just don't understand *our* needs. I read about it every single month in *Modern Woman,* and it's *so* true."

Running his hands through his thick, tousled brown hair, Nick scoffed at her. "You don't need makeup! Who's crazy enough to bring mascara on a sailing trip?"

"Give me a little credit, Nick," Jessica snapped. "It's waterproof!"

Angrily shoving a few bags on top of one another, Nick climbed into the backseat. "You're not taking all of these bags, Jessica. I'll tell you that right now. So start figuring out which ones you want and which ones you'll be sending back with your sister."

Elizabeth glanced at Nick in the rearview mirror and then over at Jessica, who'd slid into the seat beside her and slammed the door shut. Her pale lips were drawn back tightly against her teeth. Elizabeth could tell that her sister was fighting to keep her cool, but she didn't want to say anything to comfort her at the moment— not with Nick acting so strangely.

The air in the Jeep settled into a thick and heavy silence as Elizabeth pulled out of the police parking lot and headed toward the marina. The condescending tone of Nick's voice made Elizabeth's fingers tighten defensively around the steering wheel. *No one talks to my sister that way,* Elizabeth growled silently, trying to keep the words from jumping off the tip of her tongue. She was seething, ready to pounce on Nick if he decided to berate Jessica again in even the slightest way. It didn't matter how unreasonable Jessica was being—Elizabeth would stand by her twin no matter what.

Elizabeth was so lost in thought, she almost missed a stoplight. Suddenly she found herself worrying about leaving Jessica alone with Nick for the entire week. What if he lost his temper and did something stupid?

Don't obsess about it, whispered a tiny voice in the back of Elizabeth's head. *Nick's a good guy. He's a cop—you know he'd never do anything to hurt Jess. He's probably just had a bad day, that's all. As soon as he gets out on the water and relaxes he'll be back to normal. Jessica will be fine.*

Even though she wanted to believe everything would be all right, Elizabeth couldn't seem to get rid of the fears that floated around in her head like tiny, dark storm clouds. And they would keep nagging at her to miserably until she could be sure that everything was going to be OK.

"Um, is there a phone on the boat, just in case I need to call you?" Elizabeth asked, shattering the silence.

"No," Nick answered gruffly.

"Nick has his cell phone," Jessica said as if he weren't there.

"I don't want to bring the phone," he interrupted. "I don't want anyone from the precinct calling me."

Elizabeth steered the Jeep down the narrow, cobblestoned side street that led to the marina. "You really should have something just in case there's an emergency," she ventured delicately.

"There's a radio on the boat. That's all we need." In the mirror's reflection Elizabeth watched as Nick reached into the pocket of his black leather jacket and pulled out the cell phone. He handed it to her through the space between the two front seats. "Do me a favor, Liz. Could you please hold on to this until we get back?"

"Sure," Elizabeth answered hesitantly. She popped open the hidden compartment beneath the armrest and dropped the phone into it,

11

slamming the lid shut. No one said another word.

When they reached the marina, there were no parking spaces to be found anywhere. Cars were jammed along the narrow streets leading to the waterfront. It seemed as if everyone in Sweet Valley had spontaneously decided to spend the afternoon boating. And it was no wonder—the sky was a brilliant, crystal blue and the water was as smooth as glass. Elizabeth tilted back her head and breathed in the pungent, salty air pouring in through the Jeep's open top.

"Stop right here," Nick suddenly ordered.

Elizabeth brought the Jeep to an abrupt and illegal halt, blocking the entrance to Pirate Perry's Pleasure Crafts & Marina. Stealing a sidelong glance at her sister, Elizabeth watched as Jessica's upper lip curled in distaste at the enormous inflatable parrot wearing an eye patch that hovered over the yacht rental office.

Nick climbed out of the back. "I'll go in and check on our charter while you two unload." He turned toward Jessica and gave her an apparently meaningful glare. His icy expression had hardly melted at all since they had left the station. "You can only take two bags, Jess. That's it."

Jessica's expression soured as she watched him walk away. *"You can only take two bags, Jess.*

That's it!" she mimicked, her voice not unlike what Elizabeth imagined the inflatable parrot might have sounded like if it could talk.

Silently the twins got out of the Jeep and faced the seemingly impossible task of sorting through Jessica's luggage. After pushing the driver's-side seat forward, Elizabeth touched a few pieces gingerly, just to show Jessica she was willing to help. But Jessica began picking up her bags and throwing them down on the floor of the Jeep angrily, as if she had no intention of making up her mind.

Elizabeth cleared her throat, almost afraid to ask the question ready to burst out of her. "Look, about Nick . . . is everything O—"

Jessica stamped her feet on the ground angrily. "Nick is being *such* a creep!"

"I agree, Jess. He's obviously got something on his mind. But I don't want him taking anything out on you. Honestly, are you two going to be all right?"

"I'll be fine, really. But . . . it's just that I've never seen him act like this before. Maybe he'll lighten up when we get out to sea."

I sure hope so. Anxiety continued to gnaw quietly at Elizabeth's stomach, and the thought of Jessica not being able to reach her if she was in trouble only made it worse. Elizabeth bit the inside of her cheek and looked away, not wanting her twin to see the worried shadows that darkened her eyes.

Despite Elizabeth's efforts, Jessica seemed to be able to read her thoughts. "What if Nick and I fight the whole time? I'll go crazy being out in the middle of the ocean with no one to talk to." As if seized with a sudden inspiration, Jessica looked over her shoulder, then popped the secret compartment lid and slipped Nick's cell phone into her makeup bag. "This ought to do the trick."

Elizabeth cheered silently to herself. "What will Nick say?" A slow grin slunk across Jessica's face. "He can't say anything if he doesn't know."

Elizabeth helped heave the last of Jessica's four bags onto the rented yacht. "Now, for the last time—"

"Am I sure I'm going to be OK?" Jessica finished for her with a giggle. "Of course, Liz. I'm going to do everything in my power to make sure this turns out to be the best vacation ever. I'm sure I'll have plenty of great stories to tell you when I get back."

Jessica hoped she came across convincingly enough to her sister. Sure, she knew deep down in her heart of hearts that Nick would come around as soon as the shore disappeared out of sight. With nothing to defend himself against her arsenal of charms, how could he resist? But there was something about her sister's overly concerned tone that was making Jessica—who was quite possibly the most spontaneous and impulsive woman on the planet—actually second-guess herself, if only for a moment.

"How many bags have you got over there, Jess?"

Jessica shot a quick glance over her shoulder in the direction of the voice. There Nick stood on the far side of the yacht, in the midst of preparing for departure. His face was difficult to read in the bright sunshine; his sunglasses masked his expression. But his voice already sounded less edgy and harsh than it had just an hour earlier.

"Four," Jessica blurted without thinking. He had given her a two-bag limit, after all. Wincing, she braced herself for Nick's inevitable verbal onslaught.

But Nick only shook his head in response, and Jessica was sure she could hear him chuckling. "It's better than eight," he replied softly.

Jessica's heart gave a quick, triumphant leap. "You see, Liz? Everything's going to be just fine."

Her sister raised one eyebrow, then nodded. "OK, OK. It's an improvement, at least. A very *small* improvement, but an improvement all the same." She leaned forward and wrapped her arms around Jessica in a big hug. "Be good, Jess. I'm going to miss you, believe it or not."

"Oh, I believe it," Jessica quipped, hugging her sister right back. "I'll miss you too."

Elizabeth gave Jessica one last, final squeeze and stepped away. "Now, if any emergency comes up, or if Nick starts acting weird again, or if you ever need to talk—"

"I'll know where to find you." Jessica patted her makeup bag, where she'd stashed the cell phone, and winked. "Don't worry, Liz. The only calls you'll get will be from me bragging about what a great time I'm having."

"I sure hope so," Elizabeth said quietly before turning and heading back toward the beach.

Jealous much? Jessica replied silently. She appreciated her sister's concern but couldn't stand it when Elizabeth insisted on being the cloud blocking out her sunshine. *Well, it's nothing but blue skies from here on in,* Jessica told herself, shielding her eyes from the sun as she waved good-bye to Elizabeth. *This is going to be the most romantic getaway ever, and nothing—I mean* nothing—*is going to get in our way!*

Chapter Two

"Jessica! Come up here for a minute!" Nick called from the deck as he motored the *Halcyon* out to sea. The name meant tranquility, and from the very moment Nick pulled away from the dock, he felt a cool inner calm flow through his body like the crested blue waves of the ocean. He couldn't get away fast enough from the place that had made his life a chaotic nightmare for the last few weeks. Kicking the engine into high gear, Nick took one last look at the hilly green coastline before turning to face the vast, clean Pacific gloriously stretched out before him.

Jessica emerged from the cabin barefoot, finally rid of the ridiculous high-heeled shoes she had insisted on wearing. A sweater was tightly wrapped around her shoulders, and she rubbed her arms as if she were cold. Nick grinned inwardly, glad that Jessica finally understood why he insisted she only bring the necessities. He wasn't trying to be mean—just practical.

"There's a kitchen down there, an eating area, and two bedrooms!" Jessica said excitedly as she wobbled across the rocking deck. Nick knew it would take her a little while to find her sea legs, high heels or no high heels. "There's even a cute bathroom with a little vanity."

"Head," Nick said, cutting the engine.

"Huh?"

"The bathroom on a boat is called a *head*."

"That's nice," Jessica answered dryly. "Am I going to be quizzed later on every part of the boat?"

Nick gave the rigging one last check. "Nope. But I *am* going to quiz you on how to sail it. Ready for a crash course?"

Tilting her head toward the fading sunlight, Jessica wrinkled her nose. "It really sounds tempting, Nick, but I noticed that there's a VCR and a few movies in the front room—"

"*Berth*," Nick gently corrected for a second time. He was beginning to feel like a fussy old college professor.

"*Whatever.*" Jessica exhaled. "Anyway, I thought I'd check that out and maybe take a nap." Delicately she turned on her red-tipped

18

toes and headed for the narrow cabin stairs. "I'll see you in a little while. Have fun."

Nick's jaw clenched involuntarily and his shoulders sagged a fraction of an inch. As much as he loved Jessica and wanted her to have a good time, there was absolutely no way he was going to do all the work by himself. It was his vacation too, after all.

"I'm not asking, Jess. You need to learn how to sail. We're going to do this together."

Jessica stiffened. Deep creases furrowed her brow—a sign Nick found as ominous as black clouds on the horizon. "What is your problem, Nick?" Jessica demanded. "I'm sorry, but the technicalities of sailing don't interest me."

"I'm sure they'll interest you if there's an emergency." Nick fought to keep his voice civil as the muscles in his back and shoulders wound themselves as tight as the rope he was holding in his hands. "You need to learn how to sail in case something happens to me."

"Nothing's going to happen to you," Jessica said gently, her blue-green eyes softening. The way the sun played off her beautifully soft skin made Nick tremble inside. No matter what Jessica did, Nick found it impossible to stay angry at her for very long.

"This is a vacation, not a stakeout, Nick," she reminded him, drawing closer.

19

But if I handle a boat as badly as I handled the kidnapping case, we're in a lot of trouble, Nick thought, his chin dropping to his chest.

Jessica stroked the back of his neck with the tips of her fingers. "Nick, what's the matter?"

"Nothing," Nick answered quickly, feeling a heavy weight return to the center of his chest. Trying to push away the feelings of shame that were threatening to resurface, Nick forced a smile. "It's just that the wind is coming onto the bow and we should get the mainsail up."

Jessica reached for the main halyard rope in resignation. "OK, Nick, I give up. How do you work this thing?"

As soon as the blue mist of dusk began to settle around the *Halcyon,* Jessica retreated into the cabin to find something to make for dinner. In the kitchen, or "galley," as Nick so insistently called it, she could hear Nick's footsteps on the deck above as he prepared the boat for the night.

Jessica clicked a switch above the tiny sink and examined her hands under the dim galley light. Her long, slender fingers were swollen and blistered from the countless times Nick made her practice raising and lowering the sails. To make matters even worse, her manicure was totally ruined.

This is hardly the romantic vacation I had in mind, Jessica sulked silently as the floor gently pitched and rolled beneath her feet. Nick was so into sailing the stupid boat, it was as if he'd forgotten that she was even there. The only attention he paid to her was when he was teaching her to sail. Every time she'd try to break Nick out of his all-work-and-no-play mode by wrapping her arms around him and nuzzling him in that little place behind his ear—something that usually *never* failed to drive him crazy—he'd stubbornly continue barking out directions like a frustrated tutor.

Lucky for you, Nick, I don't give up so easily. Jessica pulled herself together with a determined air, a sly smile curving the corners of her mouth. *By the time this evening is over, Captain Fox, you won't know port from starboard.*

"Step number one—a cozy dinner for two." Jessica hummed contentedly to herself as she opened the narrow white cupboard doors in search of ingredients for a delicious and romantic meal. She couldn't wait to wow Nick with an elegant pasta dish or maybe even Elizabeth's favorite recipe for lemon-pepper chicken—not that she even had a clue how to make either one. But Jessica knew better than anyone that being madly in love made anything possible.

How hard can cooking be anyway? Jessica

wondered. *You just throw a bunch of stuff together in a bowl and microwave it for a couple of minutes.* Besides, if she ran into serious trouble, her sister, Elizabeth, the cooking wizard, was only a stealthy cell-phone call away.

"Hmmm . . . this *can't* be right . . . ," Jessica murmured as she peered into the cupboard. She pushed aside cans of beans and soup only to find even more cans of beans and soup stacked all the way to the top shelf. In the corner she discovered four cans of tuna, two packets of Jell-O, and some canned spaghetti with meat-balls.

"Dog food," Jessica grumbled, wrinkling her nose, but her stomach growled in rebellion. The galley was starting to feel smaller and more confining with every moment that passed. Maybe Nick didn't have a problem spending a week moping on a floating prison, but Jessica was going to go out of her mind if things didn't improve soon.

"Eenie, meanie, minie, moe . . ." Jessica tapped a jagged fingernail against the top of the cans until finally the can of tomato soup won out. Her sore hands struggled with the manual can opener for several minutes, accompanied by angry grunts and violent thoughts. Finally she got the stupid thing open, and she pried off the top with a knife, careful not to splatter tomatoey goo all over her white halter top.

"Now I know what it must've been like to live in the Stone Age," Jessica thought aloud as she dumped the thick red soup into a plastic bowl. "But at least I've got a microwave. Thank you, modern technology."

While dinner cooked, Jessica slipped into the berth to put part two of her plan into motion. Rifling through her bags, Jessica hunted for the perfect outfit to steer Nick's attention away from the boat and toward her. Socks, T-shirts, and shorts flew behind Jessica as if she were a dog digging for an old buried bone. But at last she found her treasure—the one extravagance she had managed to smuggle past Nick's watchful eyes. It was a royal blue satin kimono.

Jessica slid her arms into the smooth, cool sleeves and tied the sash around her waist. After a few coats of mascara, a bit of pale pink lipstick, and a wild toss of her long blond hair, Jessica gave her reflection in the round porthole mirror an impressed smile. *I should write a book,* Jessica thought with a proud sigh. Instant Evening Wear in a Crisis, *by Jessica Wakefield*. If this didn't pull Nick out of his funk, nothing would.

Jessica took the bubbling bowl of soup and placed it on a tray with a box of crackers she found near the sink. Carefully she carried the dinner up the steps to the deck, shifting her weight from side to side to counteract the rocking of the boat.

"Dinner's ready!" Jessica called, stumbling a little on the top step. The sun was well below the horizon now, leaving the world in total blackness. In the inky dark Jessica couldn't see the mast or the sails or even where the boat ended and the ocean began. She could only hear the loud slap of the wind against the luffing sails and the sound of the water as the bow of the boat cut through the waves.

Fear gripped Jessica's stomach as she stood frozen, her eyes darting wildly in the dark. She had absolutely no idea where to go, if her next step would send her plunging overboard. "Nick! Where are you?" she cried as she gripped the tray with trembling hands.

"I'm over here," Nick called. His voice sounded only a few feet away from where she was standing.

"Where?" Suddenly Jessica saw the glow of a lantern appear, its light flickering across Nick's handsome face. He was smiling at her. Yes—he was finally smiling!

Jessica carefully hustled over to her boyfriend and set the tray on the small deck table while Nick steered the boat on a starboard tack. As the boat turned, the sails quieted as they filled with air.

"Watch out for the boom," Nick said, pointing to the long, horizontal wooden pole that held down the mainsail. The boom swung freely across the deck as the boat shifted direction. "If that thing hits you, it could knock you out."

The boom isn't the only thing that'll knock you out, Jessica teased silently, relaxing as she felt the caress of satin against her skin. But when she looked down to admire her outfit, Jessica nearly cried out in frustration. In the pitch-black of the Pacific night, her carefully chosen outfit could hardly even be seen.

"What's for dinner?" Nick asked softly as he slid in the seat next to Jessica. He latched the lantern down securely in the center of the table and peered down at the dimly lit bowl. "Did you make Jell-O?"

Jessica groaned inwardly. "It's tomato soup."

"I love tomato soup," he answered good-naturedly, stirring it with a spoon. "It seems a little on the thick side, Jess. Did you remember to add water?"

Water? Jessica cringed in the dark as all her hopes for a romantic vacation quickly jumped ship. *Why can't one thing go right? Just one, please?*

"It's OK." Nick leaned over and kissed Jessica softly on the lips, melting away her disappointment. He reached for a cracker and dunked it into the bowl as if it held thick, smooth salsa. "This is what boating is all about—adventure. Adventure and roughing it."

"It's more adventure than I need." Jessica giggled lightly, resting her head on Nick's strong shoulder. "And a little rougher than I expected."

Jessica gasped in wonder when she looked up for the first time and noticed the thousands of stars over their heads. In all her life Jessica had never seen so many. They were as bright and sharp as chipped crystal, forming a dome above them that seemed to follow the curve of the earth.

"It's beautiful, isn't it?" Nick asked, kissing her temple.

Jessica turned to face him, her chest swelling with warmth when she saw his easy, gentle grin and his jade green eyes shining lovingly through the darkness. "I don't know what's more beautiful," Jessica whispered teasingly, her body growing limp with relief that Nick's gloomy mood had disappeared with the sun. "The sky . . . or seeing you smile again."

"Oh, Jess . . ." Nick leaned in and brushed his lips against her mouth tenderly before locking them onto hers with a tingling kiss. Jessica surrendered happily to his embrace, tracing a fingertip along his strong, chiseled jawline.

Their kisses quickly grew more passionate, and Jessica had to break away to catch her breath, her heart pounding dangerously fast.

"Mmm . . . now this is what I call a vacation," Jessica cooed, snuggling against the warmth of Nick's chest. She hoped the romance of the moment would never end. For once there would be no emergencies at the police station or phone calls to take him away. For the first time ever, Nick was all hers. "This is so nice."

"What is?"

"Having your undivided attention for once." Jessica's lips traveled along the side of his neck. "You've been so distant lately."

Nick's fingers massaged Jessica's shoulders. "I'm so sorry, Jess. The Horstmueller case was really wearing on me."

"Here, let me," Jessica said, gently removing his hands so she could do the same for him. It wasn't an easy task; despite their long embrace, the muscles in Nick's neck and shoulders were so clenched that the effort pained her already sore fingers. "Why are you so tense, then? The Horstmueller case is all over, right? Now you can forget about it and relax."

Nick drew in a deep breath. "No, Jess," he began hesitantly. "It's not all over . . . that's the problem. I haven't told you the whole story."

Pulling her hands away, Jessica watched

shadows crease Nick's face in the lantern light. "What haven't you told me?"

Nick was silent for several seconds before he spoke again. "First of all, this trip isn't exactly a vacation—it's a forced leave of absence. I had no choice."

Jessica swallowed hard. "Chief Wallace didn't fire you, did he? He can't! You're the best cop on the force!"

"Not anymore," Nick muttered, tilting his head against hers. "He didn't fire me, exactly; he just told me to take a break for a while until I got a chance to sort things out."

"Sort what out?" Jessica sat up and stared at Nick, but he refused to meet her gaze. "What happened, Nick?"

Nick's voice grew raspy, as if he were trying to hold back a flood of emotion. Jessica reached for his trembling hand. "I messed up big time," he said. "We were about to crack the Horstmueller case and I blew it. It happened right at the drop-off, when Vincent Horstmueller was about to hand over the ransom for his daughter. My team was waiting near the drop-off point, and I don't really know what happened . . . I jumped too soon, I guess. The kidnapper must've spotted me because he high-tailed it out of there without trying to collect the ransom. Now we're right back where we started. Katherine Horstmueller is still being held captive, and it's all my fault."

"Oh, Nick, that's terrible. . . . I'm so, so sorry." Jessica was at a loss for anything more to say, knowing that there were no words that could bring Nick comfort. She was relieved to know why Nick was in a rotten mood, but the knowledge made her heart ache all the same. Nick was a great cop—the best. Jessica was sure that his error had been an honest mistake, but there was no way to convince him of that, not when he thought he had done something wrong. Chief Wallace probably felt the same way. As Nick's boss he probably knew just as well as Jessica did that no one was harder on Nick than himself.

"You should have seen the look on Mrs. Horstmueller's face when we told her—" Nick's voice broke. "I swear I'll never forget it. Not as long as I live."

Jessica cradled Nick's head in her arms. "I'm sure everything will turn out fine in the end, Nick. You have to believe that."

The corners of Nick's eyes were damp with tears. "If something happens to her, Jess, I don't think I'll be able to live with myself."

"Nick . . ." Jessica felt tears welling up inside her. It almost killed her to see Nick so vulnerable. As Nick wrapped his arms around her and broke down, Jessica did the same. They held each other tight, tighter, the ocean's quiet roar ebbing and flowing in time with their sobs.

Minutes—it could have been hours—passed, and Nick sat up suddenly, his face set with determination. Jessica reached forward and brushed the remaining tears from his eyes. Snatching her hand away, Nick kissed Jessica's fingertips gently. She closed her eyes, letting the gentle pressure of his lips soothe the lingering ache from the day's hard labor.

"Listen, Jess," Nick began, "let's not let anything get in the way of us having a good time, OK? No more talk about the case or the outside world, for that matter. From here on in, we're on vacation. It's just you and me, together. Alone."

Jessica sniffled and grinned in spite of her tears. "You don't know how long I've been waiting to hear you say that," she breathed as she felt Nick's strong hands cup her face, his kisses raining down upon her as if they would never end.

Chapter Three

A flock of seagulls swooped overhead, circling the patch of early morning sky just above the white frothy wake of the *Halcyon* as if they had just spotted a school of fish. Nick filled his lungs with the cold sting of Pacific air and secured the lure and steel leader to the fishing line. With a light flick of the wrist he cast the line and watched as it trailed along behind the boat, bound to catch something along the way.

A solid, comfortable feeling settled deep in Nick's bones; he looked forward to having fresh fish for dinner that night. All he had to do was sit back, relax, and enjoy the smell of the strong salt air, the comforting rays of the sun, and the tranquil rhythm of the waves. For the sake of his sanity—and Jessica's—he swore he wouldn't think about anything else but the fish that were going to wind up on the end of his line.

"Nick, is there anything to drink around here besides water?"

Turning in his deck chair, Nick saw that Jessica had popped her head out of the cabin, her puffy eyes blinking in the harsh sunlight. He felt his chest deflate slightly in disappointment that his moment of peaceful silence had been broken.

Why is Jessica up so early? he wondered to himself. *She hates to get up before noon.*

"Nick, I'm really thirsty."

"Check the berth—I brought a few bottles of juice."

Jessica's head disappeared below deck and Nick returned to concentrating on his fishing pole. Settling back, he watched the orange and gold rays of the sun spread across the blue-green crests of the waves like a giant hand grasping the world in its fingers. Sunlight tingled on his skin in between cooling gusts of wind.

"I can't find it," Jessica called again. "Where did you say it was?"

"In the berth," Nick repeated, refusing to move from his spot. "It should be in a plastic grocery bag somewhere."

The peaceful silence returned, leaving Nick to surmise that Jessica had gone below again for a second look. He was watching the gray-and-white wings of the gulls coasting on the air when suddenly he felt a tug on his line. Securing his grip on the fishing rod, Nick sat up and waited. There it was again. Unmistakable. He had caught something.

Anchoring himself in his chair, Nick gave the reel a few turns, then waited a few beats before reeling in again. The tugging was harder and more distinct this time, and Nick had a feeling it was probably a good-size fish. The seagulls hovered closer to the water and Nick reeled hard, the line pulling so taut that the rod arced like a bow.

"I can't find the juice!" Jessica hollered, her voice taking on a whiny edge.

Nick gritted his teeth and pulled. "I can't come right now . . . I'm reeling one in!"

The soft sound of Jessica's feet padding across the deck came up behind him. She leaned on the railing in front of him and planted herself there as she slipped on a white terry cover-up over her purple one-piece swimsuit. "I looked all through your stuff, and I didn't see it. Are you *sure* you brought some juice?"

The veins in Nick's forearms bulged as he strained against the fish. He let the line out again a few yards, then reeled again as fast as he could. It was the absolute wrong time for him to have to think about a few bottles of juice.

"Maybe you put it somewhere else. Can you remember where?" Jessica's toes tapped impatiently against the deck as she stared at him, seemingly unaware of the battle Nick was waging.

Jessica's question made Nick hesitate for a fraction of an instant, just enough time for the fish to gain an edge. Nick grunted loudly, using the muscles in his legs to pull the rod back. But Jessica's heavy stare was splintering his concentration.

"I'm totally parched, Nick. Jeez, aren't you even listening to me?"

Nick's fingers were slippery with sweat. "I'll help you in a second. Let me just bring this guy in. . . ." His face was growing hot under the ever-increasing strain. Nick was starting to think this was going to be the biggest fish he'd ever caught in his life.

"Never mind," Jessica answered testily. "I'll find it myself."

In the brief moment Nick turned his head to watch Jessica stalk off to the other end of the deck, the fish gained momentum, snapping the line in two and taking his steel lure along with it. Nick's fishing rod sprang back with a jerk, a broken line dangling at the other end. No sooner was the battle lost than several of the seagulls hit the water, each one making off with a flapping silver fish in its beak.

Cursing, Nick threw his rod down on the deck and slammed his hand against the rail. "Well, there goes dinner," he muttered.

"Don't make such a huge deal out of it, Nick. There are billions of fish out there. You have all day to get another one!" Jessica finished off her glass of orange juice and watched Nick sulk over the fish he lost.

Why do guys have to make such a big deal over stuff like that? she wondered as she picked up a nail file and started smoothing out her rough fingertips. Last night, when Nick had confided in her about the botched sting, she thought it would put an end to his moodiness. Now she was starting to think it was only the beginning.

"What I want to know is why you couldn't have waited five minutes," Nick ranted. He turned on his portable waterproof radio and tuned in a football game. "Have a little patience. Why does everything have to be *now, now, now?*"

Jessica put down the file. A lump formed in her throat. "I don't like it when you talk to me that way, Nick," she said, her voice wavering. "Just because things went wrong with your job—"

"Can we *please* not talk about that?" Nick shouted above the noise of the radio. "I thought we made a promise—"

"But you also promised that we were going to have a good time!" Jessica clicked off the radio, a mist of tears springing to her eyes. "Honestly, you never want to talk to me about anything! You keep everything to yourself, leaving me wondering half the time what's going on with you. I mean, when you were all moody and stuff yesterday, I kept thinking it had something to do with *me,* not the Horst—"

"Enough!" Nick leaned against the railing and seemed to regain his calm for a moment, but the hard line of his jaw gave him away. "This is a vacation, Jess," he said slowly. "I need this time to unwind, not to work on our relationship."

Jessica stood up, her fists clenched. "So you want me to shut up and not tell you how I feel? Is that it?"

Nick's eyes suddenly grew wide and he pointed toward her. "Duck!" he shouted.

Duck? Jessica was caught off guard for a brief instant, wondering why Nick would look so surprised over seeing a stupid duck. Jessica had turned her head to look where he was pointing when suddenly the wooden boom swept across the deck and smacked right into

Jessica's forehead, laying her out against the deck. She curled up in a fetal position as hot, searing pain surged through her. When Jessica opened her eyes, she saw Nick standing over her, his green eyes filled with worry.

"Oh no, Jess; I tried to warn you . . . ," he whispered, holding out his hand to help her up.

Jessica's eyes stung with tears of pain and humiliation as she slapped his hand away. "Leave me alone, Nick!" she cried, getting to her feet and blindly finding her way to the stairs. "I don't need any more of your help!"

"Oh no, not now." Elizabeth groaned. She was just putting the finishing touches on her art history term paper on abstract expressionism when the telephone started ringing. She paused for only a moment before she decided to ignore the phone and continue typing away on the computer keyboard.

Elizabeth couldn't let anything break her concentration, not when she was on the verge of explicating how Willem de Kooning's *Woman II*, while being a vile affront to the senses on a purely feminist level, could also be seen as a fascinating synthesis of analytical and synthetic cubism. Whenever Elizabeth found herself deeply entrenched in a subject, it usually took nothing short of a national emergency to drag her away.

Even then she'd put up a tough fight.

Unless, of course, it involved Jessica.

"She just left yesterday—she couldn't be calling me now," Elizabeth said aloud, feeling her mind beginning to slip out of focus. Gathering her resolve, Elizabeth resumed typing despite the insistent ringing of the phone. Whoever it was could just leave a message and deal with it.

"Hellooo. You have reached the palatial Wakefield estate," Jessica's recorded voice chimed. *"We're far too busy to take your call right now, but please leave a message and one of our people will get back to you."* The answering machine beeped.

"Liz—Liz, it's me, Jess. . . . If you're there . . ."

Elizabeth reached for the phone at breakneck speed. It only took an instant for Elizabeth to recognize the deep, mournful tone that colored her sister's voice whenever she was upset. "Jessica, what's wrong?" she said urgently.

"I'm so glad you picked up," Jessica whimpered. "It's awful, Liz—just awful. . . ."

A tingle of panic crept up Elizabeth's spine. *You knew this was going to happen,* her conscience whispered. *You should've never let your sister get on that boat.*

Elizabeth sat on the edge of her chair, poised to take action at a moment's notice. "Are you crying? What happened?"

"Nick . . . we had a . . . a fight," Jessica

38

muttered almost incomprehensibly. She was definitely crying. "My head hurts."

Hurts? Elizabeth clutched the headset so tightly, her knuckles were turning white. "Are you all right? He didn't hurt you, did he?"

Jessica sobbed into the phone but said nothing Elizabeth could understand.

Elizabeth pressed the receiver close to her ear, trying to make out her twin's muddled speech. "He said duck. . . ." Her words dissolved into wrenching cries. "This isn't . . . what I thought it would be. . . ."

"Jessica, listen to me—are you all right? Are you safe?"

"I'm in the berth. . . ."

"Good." Elizabeth paused to take a quick assessment of the situation. If she reacted purely on the emotion of the moment, Elizabeth knew she'd be likely to call the Coast Guard, the Navy, whomever or whatever it would take to make sure Jessica wasn't harmed. But history reminded her that even though Jessica sounded absolutely terrible, she *was* prone to drama and might be exaggerating a very harmless situation.

But is it harmless or real? Elizabeth wondered. *I have no way of knowing.*

But more important, was she willing to risk the possibility that Jessica was right for once?

"Take a deep breath, Jessica, and listen

closely, OK?" Elizabeth chewed her bottom lip thoughtfully.

"OK." Jessica breathed heavily into the receiver. "Wait—I think I hear him on the stairs. . . . I don't want him to know I have the phone. . . ."

What should I do? Elizabeth's fingers trembled. "Jessica, look. Stay where you are. I'll think of something—"

"I have to go . . . ," Jessica said in a hoarse whisper. "The phone . . . he'll kill me if he finds out I have it."

"Call me as soon as you've calmed down, OK? So I know you're all right. . . ." Elizabeth waited patiently for one last word from her sister. But there was only silence and then a click as the line disconnected.

"Jessica, what are you doing in there?" Nick pounded his fist against the thin, wood-paneled door of the berth.

The slim silver door handle turned, and Nick stepped aside as the door swung slowly open. Jessica stood in the doorway, staring at him with big, wet, swollen eyes and her hand still rubbing her forehead.

A cold shudder rippled through Nick's torso and pooled at his feet. "Are you all right?" he muttered gently, holding out his hands to her. "You really gave me a scare."

Jessica sniffled and gave him a sullen nod. Stepping forward, she sheltered herself in his waiting arms. "I feel so stupid."

"It was an accident. There's nothing to feel bad about." Nick carefully grazed his fingertips over Jessica's forehead, feeling the egg-shaped lump where the boom had made its contact. He brushed a few locks of hair over it. "It's happened to me dozens of times."

The corners of Jessica's mouth turned up slightly as she wiped her tear-stained cheeks with the back of her hand. "It's not just that . . . it's the whole trip. We've gotten off to such a bad start. Can't we turn around and start over again?"

Nick kissed the top of Jessica's head. He knew exactly how she felt. One of the things he loved about being with Jessica was that most of the time, life was smooth and easy when they were together. But when things went wrong, they made up for it in a big way.

"Let's go up on deck so I can take a better look at that bump," Nick said, leading Jessica by the hand into the bright morning sunlight.

Jessica took a seat at the bow, her face to the wind and her shining blond hair blowing behind her like golden ribbons. Nick made an ice pack for her using a plastic grocery bag and a few ice cubes from the cooler they kept on deck. His heart felt heavy in his chest, as if he'd been responsible for Jessica getting hurt. Even though Nick knew he wasn't directly to blame, somewhere in the back of his mind he felt jinxed. The sailing trip felt doomed from the start, as if Nick's bad luck had followed him off-shore and out to sea.

You've been out in the sun too long, Fox, Nick told himself. *This trip is not cursed—things will get better. You'll see.*

"Nick, look!"

Nick raised his head to see Jessica's long, tanned arm pointing toward the port side of the boat. Shielding his eyes from the sun, Nick squinted at the sparkling water, trying to catch a glimpse of what had captured Jessica's attention.

"It's a rowboat," she said, taking the ice pack from Nick and applying it to her bruised head. "I think it's coming this way."

"Are you sure?" Nick reached for his binoculars. As he brought the powerful lenses into focus Nick saw the clear figure of a man in a small aluminum boat. He was drenched from head to toe and was wearing only a pair of blue jeans cut off just above the knee. The strong summer sun was turning the man's bare back a burning red; Nick guessed that he'd been out there rowing for quite some time. His thick, muscular arms pulled the oars powerfully through the water at a speed so furious, it was as if his life depended on it.

"Take a look at this, Jess," Nick said, passing the binoculars to her. "What do you think?"

"He certainly looks strong enough to handle it. . . . Wait—he stopped rowing, and it looks like he's spotted us. He's waving his arms and shouting something, but I can't read his lips. . . ."

Nick started the engine and steered the boat around. "We'd better get over there. The guy might be in trouble."

Jessica kept watch while Nick motored the *Halcyon* closer to the man in the rowboat. Instead of waiting for the yacht to catch up to him, the man continued rowing with a tireless energy, not once breaking his rhythm. Jessica found herself taking long glances at the way the shining droplets of seawater rolled from the man's wet black hair and down the reddened muscles that sculpted his shoulders and back.

"I see the trouble," Nick said, pulling the yacht into a wide circle around the boat. "It's that schooner right over there."

Jessica shifted the binoculars toward the horizon, where she spotted a two-masted schooner in the distance. A stream of black smoke swirled against the backdrop of the

43

creamy white sails. "It looks like there's a fire."

"Do you see anyone on board?" Nick asked.

Jessica panned across the long deck but saw no signs of anyone left behind. "I think he's the only one."

The corners of Nick's mouth drooped slightly. "I can't imagine he could sail that thing by himself."

When they were within several yards of the man, Jessica dropped the binoculars and cupped her hands around her mouth like a megaphone. "Are you all right?" she shouted.

The man dropped the oars, his small aluminum rowboat rocking in the *Halcyon*'s wake. He stood up in the boat and shook his wet black hair. *"I need help!"* he yelled, his chest heaving.

"Stay right there!" Jessica shouted back. She reached for the white flotation ring that was tied to the railing. "We'll help you!"

"Wait a second, Jess," Nick said cautiously as he cut the engine. "I don't know about this. . . . We have no idea who this guy is. . . ."

Jessica's lips pinched disapprovingly. "Stop thinking like a cop, Nick. This man needs our help. We just can't leave him out there—he's going to dehydrate. He's burning up out on the water."

"Maybe you're right, but it doesn't hurt to

be a little on the safe side," Nick argued. "Why don't we radio the Coast Guard before—"

Nick was interrupted by a yell and a splash that came from the water. Jessica's head whipped around to see the capsized aluminum rowboat and a circle of white foamy water where the man had fallen in.

Jessica didn't wait for a signal from Nick to react. Without losing a precious second, Jessica's instincts as a trained lifeguard took over as she threw the flotation device overboard then hurled herself off the deck, slicing the water with a clean, splashless dive.

The frigid, salty water sent a jolt through Jessica's limbs. She arched her back and opened her eyes to stinging blue, catching sight of the tall, muscular body sinking only a few feet from where she had landed. Jessica maneuvered behind the drowning man, wrapping one arm around his shoulders and reaching for the flotation device with her free arm. She struggled to hold his head above the surface of the water, but the man's large, slippery frame was sliding from her grip.

"Help me, Nick!" Jessica shouted breathlessly. "I'm losing him!"

Nick quickly reached for the rope that was tied to the lifesaver and pulled the two of them in toward the yacht. Jessica tightened her hold around the man's shoulders. His head dropped forward, and Jessica was afraid he might have lost consciousness. "Hang in there," Jessica told him, feeling his wet black hair against her cheek. "We're going to make it."

When they reached the ladder, Nick leaned over the edge and pulled the man up on deck, with Jessica following, panting with exhaustion. The man's eyes were closed, and he still wasn't moving. His sunburned face had turned to a ghastly white; his lips were purplish in color. He wasn't moving.

"Oh no . . ." Jessica shivered with fear and cold. Nick quickly wrapped her in a towel as Jessica began to perform CPR.

Nick knelt down beside her. "Do you think he's going to make it?" he asked.

"I don't know." Jessica put her ear against the man's lips and listened for sounds of breathing. But she heard nothing.

Chapter Four

"*Are you OK?*"

"*Can you hear us?*"

A deep, bone-shattering cough shook every cell of his body as his lungs purged the saltwater he had inhaled. The first breath stung his throat raw and he rolled over on his side, clutching at his stomach as the convulsions continued.

You make it all this way and then you almost drown, he chided himself. *Nice move.* He'd thought he was strong enough to make it to the yacht, but the second his body had hit the water, his muscles just let go.

"Are you all right?" a voice called from above.

He opened his dark, salt-drenched lashes and looked up. Kneeling over him was the gorgeous blonde in the purple bathing suit who had saved him, her silky, damp hair fanning over her shoulders. Her eyes were big and blue-green, the exact color of the water she'd just saved him from, and they stared right at him with more worry and concern than he ever deserved.

"I'm *fine*." He smiled inwardly as the goddess handed him a fresh towel. *In fact, you're pretty fine yourself,* he added silently. Sighing contentedly, he closed his eyes and then opened them again to find a guy standing over him where the blonde had been.

"Do you remember your name?" he asked.

Of course I remember my name, he thought, irritated by the blonde's sudden departure. *Do I look like an idiot to you?* He blinked a few times and sat up, smiling when he spotted the purple-suited bathing beauty in a nearby deck chair. "Sure, I know my name. . . . It's Eric. Eric Griffin."

"I'm Jessica," the blonde said.

"And I'm Nick." The guy held out his hand in greeting, and Eric shook it. "Are you sure you're going to be all right?"

Eric towel-dried his hair lightly. "I'll . . . I'll be fine. I just need a little rest. . . ."

"You should've never stood up in that boat." Jessica got up and sat down on the deck by his side. She turned her head and Eric followed her gaze, noticing that Nick was towing in the capsized rowboat by the rope. "You could've drowned."

Eric looked back at Jessica and swallowed hard, his fingertips poised in the air only inches away from her golden hair. He wanted so badly to touch it that it made his stomach ache. Jessica turned her head back toward him, and Eric quickly dropped his hand by his side.

"I know it was a dumb idea," Eric admitted. "But thanks for helping me anyway. I really appreciate it—especially after all I've been through. . . ."

Nick tied the rowboat to the yacht's ladder and took a seat beside Jessica, putting his arm around her. Eric figured Nick probably wanted to stake out his territory to avoid any embarrassing misunderstandings. *Don't worry, Nicky boy,* Eric thought with a smile. *I read you loud and clear.*

"That schooner's yours, right?" Nick asked.

Eric nodded. "I think there was a faulty propane tank connected to the kitchen stove. It blew a hole clear through the hull and started a fire in the cabin." He looked out over the horizon, where black smoke was still billowing above the deck. "I tried to pump out the water, but I couldn't keep up. I figured we had to get out of there because it was going down."

"We?" Jessica asked.

Eric nodded solemnly, his dark eyes downcast. "Me and my girlfriend, Katie . . ." His voice broke.

Nick's eyes were wide with alarm. "She's not still on the boat, is she?"

Hot tears came quickly to Eric's eyes, even more quickly than he thought they would. "I was up on deck when I felt the blast, and I ran down into the cabin—" He paused for a moment to stifle a sob. "I found Katie lying there on the floor, unconscious, her legs pinned down by the refrigerator—it had fallen over. I couldn't move it myself—" He stopped again to catch his breath.

"Take it easy," Jessica whispered comfortingly. Her big, soft eyes were welling up with tears and watching him with such heartfelt sympathy, it was hard for Eric to look away.

"I couldn't move it myself . . . and the water was rushing in. . . . I just jumped into the rowboat and tried to get some help. I didn't know what else to do. . . ." Eric covered his face with his hands. "I didn't know what else to do. . . ."

A slender, loving arm gently draped itself across the back of Eric's bare shoulders, sending electric currents of excitement through his veins. "You did the right thing, Eric," Jessica breathed in the most seductive voice he had ever heard. "You *had* to go for help."

Nick reached for his binoculars. "How long did it take you to get to us?"

"It's hard to say. . . ." Eric wiped the tears from his eyes and looked at the sun's placement in the sky. "Maybe forty-five minutes to an hour." He hung his head. "I know Katie's gone . . . I can feel it. She was in such bad shape when I left her, and there was no time . . . the water kept coming in. . . ." A strangled cry rose from his throat. "I'm so sorry, Katie!" Eric sobbed toward the sky. "I should've never left you alone . . . I should've stayed by your side until the very end."

"Don't say that," Jessica answered, her beautiful pink mouth quivering with emotion.

Eric turned toward Jessica, his muscular chest swelling with desire for her. "But that's how I feel, Jessica," he whispered softly. "I wish I was dead."

Nick watched the schooner through his binoculars. The artermast was tilting back slightly—a definite sign that the boat was on its way down to the bottom of the sea. His stomach clenched into a tight ball at the thought of the poor woman still left on the schooner. They couldn't give up on her so easily. What if she was still alive?

"All we wanted was a nice, peaceful vacation together." Eric moaned. "I never would've imagined in a million years it would turn out like this."

Nick put down the binoculars and looked over at Jessica, who was doing her best to comfort the grief-stricken man. *I'm so glad it isn't us, Jess,* Nick said silently, feeling almost ashamed for having the thought. As bad as things had seemed on the trip so far, they couldn't compare to the hell Eric had to endure. All along, while he and Jessica had been arguing, there had been another couple, just like them, sailing only a few miles away, enjoying a wonderful vacation together. And then fate dealt a deadly blow. *It could have just as easily been us, Jess. Why were we the lucky ones?* Just then Nick made up his mind about what he had to do. He turned on the engine.

Eric jumped up. "What are you doing?"

"I'm going to bring the yacht near the schooner so we can help Katie." Nick brought the *Halcyon* around, then gunned the engine.

"Wait . . ." Eric reached out and placed a heavy hand on the steering wheel. "It's too dangerous. She's already gone, I know it. You'll get yourself killed."

"You said you couldn't be sure," Nick argued. "We can't leave her there to die."

Eric's trembling lips turned white around the edges. "I'm telling you, there's no way she could've survived. Besides, there are two more propane tanks on board and I'm afraid they might explode in the fire. If we get any closer, you'll sink this boat too."

"Nick, what's going on?" Jessica asked as she strolled toward them, tying a towel around her waist.

"Nothing," Nick answered with a sigh. He cut the engine once again.

Eric released his grip on the wheel. "It's the only thing we can do, Nick. There's no point in endangering more lives." His voice grew thick. "Believe me, if there was anything I could do to save Katie, I would—but it's too late."

Nick glanced at Jessica, then at the schooner and back again. His hands slipped off the wheel. *I can't risk putting Jessica in danger,* he thought in surrender. *I'm sorry, but I just can't.*

"Did you call the Coast Guard and report the boat?" Nick asked.

Eric shook his head sadly. "There was no power in the boat, and the radio didn't work."

Nick nodded thoughtfully. "First we should get you warmed up, and then we'll call the Coast Guard." He motioned toward Jessica. "Can you get a blanket for him?"

Nodding silently, Jessica hurried down into the cabin.

"Thank you, Nick, for everything," Eric said, looking Nick squarely in the eye. "You have no idea how much this means to me."

Poor Eric, Jessica thought, her spirits leaden as she searched through the storage compartment for a thermal blanket to warm him. *He's so young and good-looking, with so much to live for. I don't know how anyone could survive a tragedy like that.*

Finding a thin blue wool blanket underneath some pillows, Jessica hugged it against her wet torso and slumped against the wall in a tired daze. *I bet his girlfriend was beautiful too,* Jessica thought sadly. She pictured Katie as a petite redhead with creamy white skin and a shy smile. *I wonder if they were deeply in love. Did they plan on getting married?*

A series of images flashed in Jessica's mind. Eric and Katie setting sail in their fabulous boat, thinking about how romantic and wonderful their vacation was going to be together. Then she saw Eric and Katie swimming in the deep blue Pacific, splashing each other playfully. Then there was Eric and Katie kissing under the velvet blanket of stars.

And then, in her mind's eye, Jessica saw the

explosion and the terrible flash of light ripping a hole through the side of the schooner. She saw Katie's small, pale body trapped beneath the debris, Eric's strong arms straining futilely as the water rushed in. . . .

"Jessica?"

The sound of Nick's voice coming from above snapped Jessica gratefully out of her horrific daydream. She ran up the steps at lightning speed, trying to shake off the bad feeling that was starting to settle in her bones.

"Here's the blanket." Jessica unfolded it and wrapped it around Eric's shivering shoulders. "What did you want, Nick?"

"Never mind." Nick leaned over the radio, pushing buttons and turning dials. "I was going to ask you to bring up my cell phone so we could call the Coast Guard, but I just remembered that I gave it to Elizabeth before we left."

Should I tell Nick the truth? Jessica wondered. She glanced at Eric, who was staring at his smoking boat with the glassy eyes of a man who'd just lost everything. *This is important,* argued a little voice inside her head. *You have to tell him.*

"Nick . . ." Jessica walked softly toward him, biting her lower lip. Nick was too busy trying to work the static-filled radio to see the pained expression on her face. "Actually, the cell phone is in my bag downstairs."

Nick looked up from the panel, his green eyes squinting in confusion. "How did it get there?"

"I put it there." Jessica braced herself for the inevitable explosion of anger.

The lines around Nick's mouth softened. He studied her for a moment with a look of irritation that gently melted into tenderness. "It's a good thing you brought it," he said, planting a sweet kiss in the middle of Jessica's furrowed brow. "We could definitely use it right now." He stepped away from the instrument panel. "I'll go get it."

Jessica smiled contentedly, letting the warmth of Nick's kiss flood through her. *I'm so lucky to have you, Nick,* she thought, overcome with the glow of love. Their lives had become so entwined, Jessica couldn't remember what life had been like before she met him. *And I can't imagine life without you either.*

The flame of Jessica's happiness was quickly snuffed out by the sight of Eric shivering beneath the blue blanket. "Can I get you something else? Do you need anything?"

"I'm fine." Eric turned his head toward her and looked at her with his deep, black, glassy eyes. Then, almost imperceptibly, he gave her a sly wink—or so she thought.

Jessica's breath caught in her throat. *I must be imagining things,* she told herself. *He couldn't be winking at me . . . a guy who just lost his girlfriend wouldn't do that. Maybe it's some sort of weird reflex from the cold water. . . .*

But Eric's stare was unrelenting—a gaze that captured her with the intensity of a man who was trying to possess her soul. Jessica looked away, unnerved. "Are you sure there isn't something I can do for you?"

"Just stand right there—right where you are," Eric said in a throaty whisper. "Please don't leave me alone."

"I won't leave you alone. I promise," Jessica said quietly, her voice soothing every jangled nerve left over from his fall. A chill ran through him, deeper than the cold ocean water.

Jessica has to be one of the most beautiful girls I've ever seen, he thought, letting his dark eyes travel the length of Jessica's slim, tanned body when she wasn't looking. *And she's one of the nicest too.* Every worried smile that curved her lips and every limpid glance from her ocean blue eyes convinced Eric that Jessica was definitely the kind of girl he could be with for the rest of his life. *If only there wasn't something getting in the way. . . .*

No sooner had the idea crossed his mind than Eric saw the obstacle to his happiness walking up the stairs, carrying a cell phone in his hand.

"Maybe you should be the one to call the Coast Guard," Nick said, passing him the phone. "You know all the details of what happened."

"Thanks, man."

"Do you know the number?"

Eric tapped the side of his head with his forefinger. "It's all up here," he said as he punched a phone number on the keypad. Squinting into the sunlight, Eric forced a smile. "Thanks again for all your help—both of you."

After a few rings there was a click on the other end of the line and then a stilted, computerized voice came on. "Thank you for calling Time and Temperature. . . . The time is exactly . . . 10:15 A.M. . . ."

Eric cleared his throat and then spoke deeply into the phone over the mechanical voice. "Yes . . . my name is Eric Griffin. . . . There's a fire on my schooner. . . ."

". . . Today's weather . . . ," the voice droned on, "clear skies . . . with a ten percent chance of an afternoon shower. . . ."

Nick handed Eric a map of the area and pointed to where they were. ". . . I think it was a propane tank. The boat is definitely going down. I was rescued by a passing boat, but there is still one person left on the schooner. . . ." Looking at the map, Eric rattled off a detailed description of the schooner's coordinates, his words falling on deaf, computerized ears.

". . . Tonight . . . skies will be cloudy. . . ."

Jessica stood close by, making Eric nervous that she might hear the monotonous speech patterns emanating through the phone and figure him out. He decided to wrap it up quickly. "Yes . . . it's very . . . urgent," he choked out through the sobs he affected in his throat. "We'll keep a lookout . . . thank you."

". . . The temperature is exactly—"

Eric clicked off the phone.

"What did they say?" Nick asked.

Eric waited until he was sure Jessica was looking, then he threw off the blanket, warming his skin in the rays of the sun. "There's another call in the vicinity . . . a more serious one."

"I wonder what happened." Jessica's frown lines grew deeper. "I mean, what could be more urgent than a girl trapped on a flaming, sinking boat? It must be something horrible."

How I would love to make you smile again, Eric thought.

"Unbelievable." Nick's shoulders slumped. "Who knows how long it's going to take for them to get here."

"The woman I spoke with said an hour or

59

two . . . maybe more." Eric drew himself up to his full height, then crossed his arms in front of him and very subtlely flexed his biceps. "I guess you're stuck with me for a little while longer," he said, casting a sidelong glance at Jessica.

"Don't worry about it, Eric. It's no problem, really," Nick answered. "We just want to make sure everything turns out for the best . . . as well as it can." He looked away, his face creased with apparent worry.

Thanks for nothing, Eric grumbled silently despite the cheerful grin on his face. *Maybe once Nick's out of the picture, Jessica and I can have some fun.*

Eric could hardly wait.

Chapter Five

"You must be quite a cook."

Jessica floated a tea bag in a mug of cold water and put it in the microwave for ten minutes. "It's just tea—" Jessica's cheeks suddenly felt warm. "Anyone can make tea."

"It's not the tea . . . it's the way you move around the kitchen." Eric leaned against the galley cupboard, close to where Jessica was standing. Perhaps just a little *too* close. "I can tell that you feel comfortable cooking."

The faint thump of Nick's footsteps sounded above their heads as he crossed the deck. Jessica tucked a loose strand of golden hair behind her ear and tried not to notice the perfect ripple of abdominal muscles that rose just above the waistband of Eric's wet cutoffs.

"I'm not a great cook, but I *can* make pretty

good soup," she mumbled, looking away. Jessica's mouth suddenly went dry and a strange, uncomfortable heat crept up her neck to her face.

"I'd love to try it sometime." Eric repositioned himself slightly so that as the boat rocked he brushed perilously against Jessica's body.

OK, what on earth is going on here? Jessica wondered uneasily. *This is definitely* not *cool.* Jessica promptly turned her back on Eric and stopped the microwave, not caring if the tea was ready or not. As Jessica turned around to hand him the mug, she caught him staring at her legs. "You'll have to settle for tea, I guess," Jessica answered sharply, suddenly feeling very self-conscious in her swimsuit.

"I'll take whatever I can get," Eric said, eyeing her through his thick, dark lashes.

Jessica carefully maneuvered herself from the ever-narrowing gap between her and Eric. "I'll be back in just a second," she said with a breathless, nervous laugh. "I'm going to change into something a little warmer."

"Don't do it on my account," Eric called flirtatiously. Jessica could feel Eric's gaze wandering all over her body as she stalked off toward the door, leaving her with a sour feeling rolling in her stomach.

This guy is really giving me the creeps, Jessica

thought, closing the door behind her. *What kind of guy loses his girlfriend in a tragic accident and then starts flirting with another girl on the same day?* The sympathy Jessica had felt for him earlier was fading into revulsion. Shaking her head in amazement, she took a pair of jeans and a white cotton T-shirt out of her bag. *Nick would be really mad if he knew that Eric was coming on to me—but what are we going to do? We just can't throw Eric back in the water and wish him good luck.* She began to peel down the straps of her wet swimsuit, her mind reeling.

"Excuse me, but . . . where would I find the sugar?"

The sound of Eric's voice nearly made Jessica jump out of her skin, clothes flying nervously out of her hands. He was standing there in the open—*open!*—doorway, seemingly pleased that he had caught her off guard.

"I'm changing! Do you *mind?*" Jessica shouted. She automatically reached for a towel to cover herself, even though her swimsuit was thankfully still in place. Her cheeks turned a deeper shade of crimson as she huffily put her shoulder straps back where they belonged. "Look, I know you've been through an awful lot today, but . . . but . . . you've got a *lot* of nerve sneaking up on me like that!"

Eric's eyebrows raised a full inch, as if he

were stunned by her outrage, yet underneath it all Jessica could tell he was extremely pleased with himself. "I'm sorry I startled you—it's just that I can't drink tea without sugar, and it was starting to get cold—"

"It's in the cabinet." Jessica thrust a pointed finger in his direction. She silently hoped Eric didn't notice how badly she was trembling. "Now get out."

"Is something wrong?" called a voice from outside the door. It was Nick.

Great, just great—now Nick is going to think I'm flirting with Eric. When Jessica dropped the towel, Eric gave her a sly wink—and this time there was no denying it was intentional. "Everything's fine, Nick," Jessica said through gritted teeth. "Just fine."

You always know how to show up at the right moment, don't you, Nick? Eric said silently. *It's one of your many talents.* He turned toward Nick with a bright grin stretched across his face to hide the bitter contempt that was lurking in his heart.

"Jessica was just about to tell me where you keep the sugar," he said, tearing himself away from Jessica's mortified stare.

"Sure—I'll get it for you," Nick answered, backing into the galley, completely unaware of what had just transpired.

I'd watch my back if I were you, Detective Fox,
Eric thought as his bare feet padded back to the
galley. *It's the little details that get you busted
every time.*

Nick handed Eric a sugar shaker and a
spoon. "I think I'm going back there," he said
decisively. "We can't just sit here and wait for
the Coast Guard to show up."

Eric sprinkled the slightest bit of sugar possible into his mug—he hated sugar. "Back
where?"

"To the schooner."

The muscles in Eric's legs and arms froze
completely still. He glanced at the half-opened
door of the cabin. This time he wasn't about to
stop him. In fact, getting Nick out of the way
was just the sort of break he should have been
rallying for all along.

"But why risk it?" Eric asked innocently,
fighting to keep his voice even. "The boat is
going down. You could get killed."

Nick ran his hands through his hair. He
looked weary. "I know," he said, exhaling his
words. "But there might be a chance that
Katie's still alive—"

"An extremely slim chance," Eric interrupted. He bit down hard on the inside of his
cheek, hoping the tears would come again.

"It's still a chance—and as long as there's a

chance we have to take it." Nick leaned against the counter, folding his arms across his chest like he was a big man.

Go for the ego—works every time, Eric thought with secret glee as he felt his eyes filling up with tears. "I can't ask you to risk your life. . . ."

"I'm a police officer, Eric," Nick answered, as if on cue. "It's what I'm trained to do."

The brave Detective Fox, always ready to fight crime when duty calls. He doesn't know how to leave well enough alone, Eric thought. *Luckily it's going to be to my benefit—not his.*

"All right," Eric conceded with a hesitant nod. "You know what's best."

"I want you to come with me."

Eric looked away. "I can't go back there!" he cried, pleased to hear his voice break. "You're asking too much of me—after all that I went through there—"

"You know the boat better than I do," Nick gently argued. His green eyes were so soft and filled with concern that it made Eric want to laugh out loud. "You can show me where everything is. . . ."

I can't go with him—that'll ruin everything, Eric told himself as Jessica suddenly appeared in the doorway. She wore the white T-shirt and jeans she had thrown from her hands so adorably when he'd walked in on her, and her long, sun-dried hair waved gloriously over her shoulders. Eric knew he'd have to dig deep to get his plan off the ground, but the sight of Jessica in all her natural beauty told him it was going to be worth it in the end.

"You don't know what you're asking!" Eric shrilled, surprising even himself with the surge of emotion that ripped from his throat. "It's too painful—"

"Katie needs you, Eric," Nick coaxed while Jessica stood motionless in the doorway. "She needs your help."

A violent shudder shook Eric's entire body. "I can't stand to see her again—like that—I'll lose my mind! I know it!" Hot tears poured freely from his eyes. "Please don't make me go back there—please . . ."

"Eric, I'm sorry I asked." Nick gave him a light pat on the shoulder. "It's all right. I'm not going to make you go there. I'll be fine on my own."

"Nick," Jessica broke in, her eyes blazing with concern. "What are you talking—"

"Be careful, man," Eric interrupted, not wanting to give Jessica a chance to protest. "I wish I could go with you . . . but it's just that—"

"You don't have to explain yourself," Nick said. "I understand perfectly."

Somehow I knew you would, Fox. Eric wiped

his damp cheeks with the back of his hand. "I feel like such a coward. . . ." His voice trailed off, as if he didn't have the strength to go on. "I'm so tired. Do you think I could rest?"

"Absolutely." Nick led him back to the cabin where Jessica had just come from. She quickly jumped aside like a little mouse and wordlessly ran up the stairs to the deck. Seeing Jessica so afraid of him made Eric feel as though his heart had just been ripped from his chest. Couldn't she see how much he liked her?

"You can stretch out on the couch if you want to take a nap," Nick said, tossing a blanket at him. "By the time you wake up, I'll probably be back. And the Coast Guard shouldn't be far behind."

Eric nodded solemnly. "Good luck," he said, shaking Nick's hand. "I hope you bring Katie back to me."

"I'll do the best I can." Nick gave a brisk, confident nod before he left, closing the cabin door behind him.

Eric settled back, smiling to himself, hands tucked behind his head. *This is just what I need—a little time to think things through*. Eric closed his eyes and listened to the sound of footsteps over his head. *You think you're infallible, Nick Fox, but you always leave a door open behind you. And I'm going to be there—waiting.*

*　　*　　*

68

"Wait a second—I have to talk to you."

Nick spun around, feeling Jessica's grip on his elbow. He was immediately confronted by her tumultuous blue-green eyes.

"You can't go," she pleaded.

"I have to, Jess," Nick answered, wrapping his arms tightly around her waist. "Katie might still be alive. After what happened with the kidnapping case, well . . . I feel like I have to make up for it somehow."

"Fine. Then take me with you. You have to."

Nick shook his head furiously. "No way. It's too dangerous."

"Not any more dangerous than letting me stay here alone with that *guy.*" Jessica's lips were pinched, and her body trembled slightly.

A feeling of unease washed over Nick like a poison trickling into his veins. Holding Jessica by the shoulders, he looked straight into her eyes. "What are you talking about?"

Jessica swallowed hard. "There's something seriously wrong with Eric. He keeps looking at me—"

"The man has just experienced an unbelievable trauma." Nick spoke in soothing tones, hoping to calm Jessica's visibly frazzled nerves. "He's in a state of shock."

"You should've seen him in the kitchen . . . he actually brushed against me." Jessica's voice rose higher and higher in pitch. "And when I was getting ready to change, he actually walked in on me! No normal man, I don't care how traumatized he is, would act like that after losing his girlfriend."

Nick's blood froze. *Did Eric really try to come on to Jessica?* he wondered anxiously. True, Jessica was extremely beautiful, but she was also prone to being overconfident of her powers of attraction. On a purely rational level it seemed highly unlikely that Eric would do those things intentionally—his grasp on reality had to be pretty warped. Yet looking down at Jessica's pale face and haunted eyes, Nick knew that it absolutely had to be the truth.

"You don't think he'll try anything, do you?" Nick asked weakly.

Jessica lowered her head and rested her cold cheek against his collarbone. "I don't want to find out."

What am I supposed to do? Nick asked himself, his gaze returning to the sinking schooner. Its black ribbon of smoke still reached toward the sky. He had to get there—soon. But the warm tickle of Jessica's breath on his neck was making it harder and harder for him to leave. The last thing he wanted was to put her in any kind of danger.

Nick gently pulled away from her. "I won't

be gone long, Jess. I promise." He turned his head and put on his sunglasses, not wanting to meet Jessica's troubled eyes. "Eric's sleeping right now. I bet I'll be back before he wakes up."

Jessica seemed hardly satisfied with the odds. "More likely he'll wake up as soon as he knows you're gone," she said dryly. "Can't we lock him in or something?"

"The doors lock from the inside." Nick reached for Jessica's hand and ventured a smile. "I work with crackpots every day, Jess. Don't you think I'd recognize one if I saw him?"

The tension lines around Jessica's lips softened just a fraction. "You're in vacation mode now, Nick. I don't think you would."

"Thanks so much for your vote of confidence," he teased. The lightness of the moment passed quickly between them as he was reminded of the gravity of the situation at hand. Nick let out a loud, tired sigh, painfully aware of the precious moments that were ticking away. "If it will make you feel any better, I can try to rig up something to keep him in there."

Jessica immediately stepped aside and extended her arm toward the stairs. "Lead the way."

Hurrying below deck and finding a wooden broom in the storage compartment, Nick slipped it through the door handle. The long end of the broom was balanced on top of the counter, keeping the pole horizontal. If Eric tried to pull the door open, the broom would smack against the wall, locking him inside.

"What do you think?" Nick whispered, working quickly and quietly so as not to disturb Eric. "It's not exactly the nicest way to treat a guest, but—"

"But it's a great way to treat a creep." Jessica tested the broom handle until she seemed positive it would hold. "It will be all right, I guess."

Nick took Jessica's hesitant answer as a green light. Scouring the boat for materials, he grabbed a fire extinguisher, the first aid kit, a hand pump to bail water, and an extra blanket. "If you run into any trouble, you can try calling me on the radio—I'm sure I can get the schooner's radio up and working. Or you can use the cell phone to call the Coast Guard."

"What's the number?"

Tearing into a vinyl envelope, Nick pulled out an orange plastic emergency raincoat and a matching set of pants. "I don't remember where it is." He pulled on the pants over his shorts and stepped into a pair of green fisherman's wading boots. "Eric called last, so hit the redial button."

"OK." Jessica bent down and tucked the

hem of Nick's plastic pants into the boots. Nick felt a lump form in his throat from the simple intimacy of her gesture. Suddenly he was reminded of how every moment they shared together was dearly precious and that it all could be cruelly taken away in the briefest of moments—just like what happened to Eric and Katie.

"You'll be all right," he said thickly, more for his own benefit than for hers. "The Coast Guard will be along soon."

Jessica settled comfortably in his arms, her head nestled under the curve of his chin. Nick was amazed at how her form always fit so perfectly in his, as if they were made for each other.

"Don't take too long," Jessica whispered, rocking in his arms. Tilting Jessica's face up toward his, Nick pressed his lips against hers in a slow, pulsating kiss. Their hearts pounded fiercely against each other through their chests, not out of pure love, as Nick hoped, but out of frightened anticipation. Pulling away, Nick's scared eyes locked onto hers. "This is going to turn out fine, Jess. I promise."

Chapter Six

Please hurry back. . . . Please hurry back. . . .

The words swirled around and around in Jessica's head like a tornado as she watched Nick's orange-clad figure row farther and farther away. The sun's rays glinted sharply off the aluminum rowboat until Nick was nothing more than a bright speck sitting on the edge of a floating silver knife. She let the image burn into her memory, just in case it was the last time she ever saw him.

Jessica sat down in a deck chair, her panicked breaths rising and falling with the waves. The water had become considerably rougher in the last hour, occasionally slapping against the side of the yacht, showering the deck with a chilling spray. Jessica recoiled.

Is the water supposed to splash this much? she

wondered, chewing nervously on a cuticle. *What if the boat capsizes?* She could hardly remember everything Nick had tried to tell her about sailing. For her entire life, Jessica had thought of the ocean as mystical and comforting—until now. Now she pictured herself on the back of a huge, scaly green dragon that thrashed violently beneath her. Jessica felt completely alone and at the mercy of its will.

"Sailing the boat is the least of your problems," Jessica mumbled to herself, wondering if Eric was still sleeping soundly below deck. Goose bumps prickled her flesh. *What's going to happen when he wakes up? Is he going to freak out that we locked him in?*

Jessica paced the length of the deck, stepping carefully so she wouldn't disturb Eric, silently counting down the minutes until Nick's return. Across the water she could see that the orange dot of Nick's suit was disappearing into the boat. Jessica clasped her hands. *Be careful, Nick. And please get back here soon.*

A tingle of anxiety started creeping up Jessica's back from the base of her spine, and her lungs contracted in spasms. Reaching for the mast to steady herself, Jessica closed her eyes and pictured Elizabeth's face, imagining what she'd say if she were standing beside her at that very moment. *"You have to stay calm and focused, Jess,"* she'd say. *"Everything is going to be fine, I just know—"*

Jessica's eyes opened suddenly, the image of Elizabeth evaporating into the salt air. She paused, listening closely.

Pound, pound, pound . . .

There it was. She wasn't imagining things. Jessica's eyes darted around the deck, hoping to find the source of the noise. It didn't matter what was making the noise as long as it wasn't Eric.

"Jessica!"

"He's awake," she whispered, her heart leaping to her throat and beating in double time. "What am I going to do?"

He's awake. . . . He's awake. . . . The words repeated themselves endlessly in her mind like a chant. Far in the distance she saw no sign of the bright neon orange of Nick's rain gear. The schooner's dull, smoky browns, whites, and greens meant he was nowhere near coming back again.

Eric's pounding grew more and more urgent, but his voice was getting softer and sweeter. "Jessica . . . where are you, Jessica? I need you."

If I don't say something, he's going to get suspicious, Jessica realized with disgust. She released the mast and glided down the stairs as if drawn by some invisible magnetic force. Standing several feet away from the door, Jessica was amazed at how well the broom handle was holding up.

"Jessica . . . are you there?" Eric called through the door. His voice was thick, as if he had been crying. "I need help, Jessica, please. . . ."

Folding her arms nervously across her chest, Jessica chewed her bottom lip. *Maybe he is sorry about what happened to Katie. Maybe I was being too hard on him.* Jessica took a step closer to the door. There wasn't any harm in at least *talking* to the guy. As long as the broom handle stayed right where it was, she'd be safe.

"What's the matter, Eric?" she said breezily, leaning against the counter. "I could hear you all the way up on deck."

"The door won't open. I don't imagine you could help me, could you?" A dark, vague tone edged his voice, leaving Jessica unsure if he was angry with her or just upset about everything that had happened with Katie.

"That stupid door!" Forced laughter escaped Jessica's lips. "I told Nick that he should fix it or one of us was going to get stuck in there."

"Try pushing on it."

"It won't do any good," Jessica lied. "The lock is broken. I'm sorry, but I can't do anything about it until Nick gets back."

Eric ceased his pounding and fell silent.

Easing herself noiselessly toward the stairs, Jessica's breaths came deeper and slower and her pulse resumed its natural beat. *It's fine,* whispered a voice inside her head. *He's not going to fight it. Everything is going to be fine.*

But just as the sole of Jessica's foot landed on the first step, a shriek came from behind the door. It was so clear and cutting that Jessica almost would've sworn that Eric had been standing next to her.

"You conniving little witch! You're lying to me!"

Shrinking back in horror, Jessica fell against the stair railing. She reached out and grasped the rail to break her fall. "J-Just wait a little while longer, Eric," she called back to him, keeping her voice as even as possible. "Nick will get you out of there. I promise."

A loud *thud* sounded, over and over again. It seemed as though Eric was slamming his entire body weight against the cabin door. The broom was starting to slide, and the thin paneled door was buckling, as if it was about to be ripped from its hinges. Jessica stood frozen, staring at the terrifying scene before her with the same numb detachment she'd have felt watching a horror movie.

"You'd better hope I don't get out of here,

Jessica," Eric panted. "Because I'm coming after you."

"Did you hear me, Jessica?" Eric pressed the side of his sweaty face against the door and listened as the hot blood pounded in his ears. Jessica didn't answer. All he could hear was the frantic *smack* of her feet as she raced up the stairs to the deck.

Eric leaned back and screamed at the ceiling, "You can't lock me up like some animal!" Flashbacks of gray cell blocks and iron bars roared through his mind at lightning speed. Eric clenched his jaw against the rapid images until he thought his teeth would break. *No one is ever going to lock me up again,* Eric swore with vengeance. *Not Jessica, not Nick Fox—no one.*

His muscles burning with invigorating pain, Eric stepped back against the far wall, and with all his fury focused on one single target, he lunged for the door. A leap in midair and then a clean, spiraling twist of the body and Eric was airborne, one graceful leg sweeping out, executing a perfect spinning side kick with the trained skill of a martial arts master. The rough heel of his foot met the weakening door with splitting agony, but Eric's leg remained rigid, disciplined. His bone absorbed the shock with the grace of a tuning fork.

It took Eric a moment to see the hole in the

door. Wiping the sweat from his eyes, he noticed the yellow straw of a broom through the jagged, splintered hollow where his foot had landed. *So that's what was locking me up,* Eric thought, laughing to himself. *For being such a good detective, Nick, you sure act like an amateur sometimes.*

Thrusting his arm through the hole, Eric yanked the broom to one side, hearing the wooden handle *clack* against the hard galley floor. Then, with an easy flick of the wrist, he pushed open the door. "Ready or not," he growled, "here I come."

As soon as Jessica heard the sharp crack of splitting wood, she knew it was over. He was coming after her—she was sure of it even before she heard Eric's heavy footsteps trudging below deck, becoming louder and more ominous with each step. To Jessica, it was like hearing the drumbeat to her own execution.

She paused by the railing for a moment, looking overboard at the white sea-foam breaking against the yacht's hull and then shifting her gaze out toward the schooner. Leaning over, Jessica contemplated making a dive for it, but her instincts told her that she'd be overcome with exhaustion before even making it halfway to the schooner. Still, the thought of

81

cold seawater filling her lungs seemed more appealing to Jessica than staying on the yacht to face a madman.

Eric's slow, menacing footsteps were making their way up the stairs to the deck. A sudden burst of adrenaline shot through Jessica's body, jerking her upright. *Don't give up,* coaxed her inner voice. *You have to protect yourself.*

Jessica spun around. *The radio,* she realized. *You can try calling Nick on the radio.* In a blurred frenzy she raced toward the radio near the steering wheel and turned it on. Two rows of buttons and dials stared back at her stubbornly, unwilling to work right until she figured out the correct combination.

Push these two buttons, then turn the first dial all the way to the right. . . . No—turn the last three dials and . . . wait. Maybe I'm only supposed the touch the buttons. . . . Maybe I wasn't supposed to touch anything at all . . . !

A cry of desperation caught in her throat and her mind went blank as she tried to remember Nick's complicated instructions. For the life of her, they wouldn't come.

The tiny hairs on the back of Jessica's neck suddenly stood up. Without even looking behind her, she instinctively knew that Eric had finally made it up on deck.

Arms flailing, Jessica pushed the button on

the mouthpiece. "Nick—Nick, are you there? Can you hear me?" The speaker crackled. It seemed to be working. Jessica pushed aside the sweaty strands of hair that stuck to her forehead and spoke again with renewed hope. "Nick, if you hear me, I need you. . . ."

"Get away from the radio, Jessica," Eric warned. His voice was deep and deadly serious.

"Nick! Help!" she continued on, feeling Eric's smoldering eyes burning into the back of her head. Her fingers squeezed the radio mouthpiece desperately. "Help! This is an emergency!"

Eric stood in front of her, the veins in his forearms bulging. "I told you to get away from there," he seethed, but Jessica wouldn't let go. It was her only hope.

"Nick!"

"The radio won't help you, Jessica. The schooner's radio is broken. And even if it wasn't . . ." With prying fingers Eric opened the side compartment and reached into the radio, pulling out a fistful of broken wires. A triumphant grin broke across his face, revealing viciously gleaming white teeth.

Jessica backed away, eyes bulging in terror, hands gripping her head. "Nick! Help me!" she screamed with such ferocity that it felt as if her lungs were on fire. *"Nick!"* But she knew with terrifying dread it was all for nothing. And when she looked out over the water, there was still no sign that Nick was on his way back.

Eric leaned casually against the mast, his grin melting into a flirtatious pout. "Don't bother screaming, sweetheart," he whispered, his stony black eyes leering at her through thick eyelashes. "No one can hear you."

The sound of Jessica's hopeless cries rose up high into the air, where they met the loud canvas slap of the mainsail before being carried off into the futile ocean breeze. As the tide of Eric's anger subsided, pity tugged at his heart at the sight of Jessica falling to her knees in surrender, tears streaming down her beautiful face.

Right now she's scared, Eric thought, listening to her broken sobs. *But as soon as she realizes how much I want to be with her, all that will change.* It wouldn't take long to convince her—Eric was sure of it. He was twice the man Nick Fox was.

"Jessica, there's something I've been wanting to tell you. . . ." Eric looked over, expecting to see Jessica's broken form lying in a puddle of tears, but instead he caught her scrambling toward the cell phone he had left on the table.

"Put that down!" Eric shouted, his blood pressure rising again. He made a move toward her.

Jessica shook her head at him. "Stay away from me, you creep!" She held out her arm to protect herself and pressed a button on the phone.

"You ungrateful little witch," Eric muttered, his feelings of affection suddenly turning bitter in his stomach. "Give me the phone!"

"I'm calling the Coast Guard," Jessica stammered, backing away from him. "They'll be here soon."

Eric paused, snickering to himself as he remembered the fake phone call he'd made earlier. "Put the phone down, Jessica," he said calmly, hypnotically. "I want to talk to you."

Jessica looked away from him, lips slightly parted as she waited in apparent hope for a Coast Guard representative to pick up on the other end of the line. Eric knew the exact moment she heard the click because her eyes suddenly lit up, but inevitably it was only seconds when the light died out again.

"You called Time and Temperature?" Jessica's voice shook with numb realization. Her arm dropped by her side. "You never called the Coast Guard?"

"I was trying to tell you, but you weren't listening to me."

Jessica's eyes darkened. "But what about the boat . . . and Katie?"

Stepping toward her cautiously, Eric slipped a strong arm around the waistband of Jessica's jeans. It made him absolutely crazy with desire to be only inches away from her honey-tinged skin and golden hair. "If you'd just relax a little bit, I can explain everything to you," he murmured tantalizingly close to her perfect ear. "Believe me, it's all for the best as far as you and I are concerned. Now why don't you just relax a little so we can get to know each other better?"

Jessica's pink mouth pinched into a scowl. "Don't touch me!" She pushed at his bare chest and backed away until she was pressed up against the railing at the bow of the yacht. With a quick finger she punched in a flurry of digits on the keypad and listened, her eyes wild.

"Liz! Thank goodness . . . I need your help—he's after me—"

"Drop the phone, Jessica." Eric's temples throbbed. He was on the edge of losing control.

Jessica's words rushed out of her in a breathless stream. "Something horrible—"

Before Jessica could even speak the next word, Eric drew his arms into position, as taut as a strung bow, then released them with a powerful fury. As if in slow motion, Eric watched as the phone flew up into the air and sailed over the railing before it splashed into the sea. Jessica's slender neck snapped to the side and she dropped unconscious to the deck floor.

Eric cursed violently, his blood roiling at the perfect plan that had somehow gone awry. "You made me do it, Jessica," he said, her body as still and lovely as Snow White's in the glass coffin. "It's your fault."

Taking one last look at the distant, sinking schooner, Eric started the yacht's engine. "Farewell, Detective Fox," he murmured, spitting into the water. "It was nice knowing you."

Chapter Seven

"Jessica . . . *Jessica!*" Elizabeth shouted hoarsely into the phone. "Can you hear me?"

There was no answer.

Knees trembling, Elizabeth sank to the edge of the bed while her mind spun wildly, trying to fit together the pieces of the puzzle that was unfolding before her.

There were shouts. . . . She must've been fighting with Nick again. . . . Jessica came on the line, hysterical. . . . He was after her. . . . Something horrible had happened. . . .

Elizabeth clutched at the bedcovers with her left hand and breathed deeply in an attempt to control the endless waves of nausea that were hitting her with brute force. There had been a strange muffled sound and then a splash—Elizabeth was certain it had been a splash—and then dead silence. The realization was enough to nearly make her heart stop.

Did Nick push Jessica overboard?

"Jessica, if you can hear me, please give me some kind of sign—just so I know you're all right. . . ."

Elizabeth waited for what seemed like an eternity, but her cries were only met with a deafening silence. "Jessica, are you there?" she shouted once more, her throat tightening painfully every time she spoke her sister's name.

Impulsively Elizabeth hung up the phone and dialed the code for number callback. *Maybe we were just disconnected, that's all,* she rationalized silently. *I'm sure that's what happened. It has to be.*

Elizabeth wiped her sweaty palms on the front of her khakis. The ringing at the other end of the line had a soothing effect on her, restoring her breathing to its natural rhythm. "She'll pick up," Elizabeth whispered to the quiet room. "I know she will."

As soon as she heard the click Elizabeth gushed into the receiver. "Jessica—we must've been disconnected. . . . What's going on? Are you—"

"I'm sorry," a tinny, mechanical voice interrupted. "The number you are trying to reach is temporarily out of service. Please try again later." *Click.*

"I can't try again later! This is life or death!" Elizabeth screamed hysterically, hurling the telephone across the room. It landed with a soft *thud* in the middle of the tangled pile of dirty clothes on top of Jessica's bed. Normally Jessica's mess infuriated Elizabeth, but now it struck an almost sentimental pang in the middle of her chest. With Jessica miles away somewhere in the vast Pacific, Jessica's things were the only tangible piece of her twin that Elizabeth had left.

I'm sorry, Jessica. I should've never let you get on that boat. I just knew something was going to go wrong.

Elizabeth paced the carpeted floor of her dorm room, reliving in her mind the last few moments before Jessica had taken off with Nick. Elizabeth had stood on the dock, waving good-bye, completely nervous and worried, while Jessica leaned against the railing of the yacht, blowing kisses like a beauty pageant contestant. Jessica's face had literally glowed with happiness, full of confidence that they were going to have a wonderful trip together. And then there was Nick, behind the steering wheel, his face serious and expressionless. As tense as he had seemed, Elizabeth would have never really believed that he was capable of violence against her sister.

Don't be so naive, Elizabeth told herself as she continued to pace aimlessly. *Violence is part of his job. It's what he knows best.* No matter how hard she tried to protect her sister, it never seemed to be enough. Terror and hopelessness slowly began to invade every cell of her body, like a rare disease, making Elizabeth feel as if she were about to disintegrate at any moment.

I can't just stand here, wondering what's happened to her, she realized, struggling to hold herself together. *I have to do something.*

Blindly Elizabeth reached for the keys to her Jeep and ran out the door, hoping a brilliant plan would come to her on the way to the marina. *Please,* she prayed in silent despair. *Don't let me be too late.*

Nick gingerly crossed the deck of the schooner in his fishing boots, pushing aside the shredded sails that dangled in his path like drying laundry. He could tell the boat was definitely sinking by the way the hull seemed immune to the motions of the increasingly rough waves. Its starboard side tilted oddly to the left so that the edge of the deck nearly touched the water's surface, while the port side rose high in the air. Nick held on to the rigging as he made his way over to the smoking bow, the ripped canvas of the sails slapping sharply in the wind. There was an eerie stillness surrounding the wrecked boat, a sort of dead calm that reminded Nick of an old merchant ship that had been looted and attacked by pirates and then abandoned to the whims of the sea.

The black ribbon of smoke he had been watching from the yacht was now dissipating, and as Nick drew nearer he could see that it wasn't nearly as bad as he had expected. Near the front of the bow were what appeared to be papers and scraps of the mainsail, as well as other refuse, in a smoldering pile.

That's odd, Nick thought, dousing out the smoky flames with an empty bucket he had found nearby and filled with seawater. *It almost looks like someone started this fire with a match.* . . . While it looked suspicious, years of police training had taught Nick never to jump to conclusions. He knew better than to make any assumptions until he had fully examined the rest of the vessel. Still, Nick was finding it difficult to ignore the weird feeling that was gnawing at his gut.

I hope I made the right decision, leaving Jessica alone with Eric, he wondered silently, stomping out the last of the flames. A strong inner voice broke through, shattering Nick's doubts. *There's a young woman whose life is in danger—you have to help her. Jessica will be just fine.*

Deep lines formed around Nick's eyes and mouth as he remembered the gravity of his purpose. With careful steps he inched along the crooked deck and found the stairs leading to the cabin below. Peering down at the dark cabin, Nick was aware only of the rising black water and the heavy scent of motor oil. Armed with his first aid kit and a flashlight, Nick lowered his body into the darkness.

Sliding his fingers along the wall, Nick toggled the light switch, but the lights didn't come on. "Eric must've turned the power off," Nick muttered. He waded cautiously through the murky, knee-deep water with only the narrow yellow beam of the flashlight as his guide.

"Katie . . . Katie, can you hear me?" Nick's voice echoed through the black cabin, mingling with the slow, liquid drips coming from a leak somewhere in the distance. Leaning forward, Nick strained to hear the slightest movement. "Katie? I'm Detective Nick Fox. . . . I'm here to help you. . . ."

Nick paused and listened, but there was no answer. He pressed on in the dark, sloshing past the large galley and the door to the engine room, heading toward the yellow disk of light aiming at one of the cabins. Nick breathed in deeply the oily fumes, filling his chest with a vague sense of doom.

"Katie?" Bracing himself, Nick pushed open the cabin door. The water flowed around his knees into the dry room. Swallowing hard, Nick scanned the room. There he found an unmade bed and piles of clothing, a few empty cereal boxes, and scattered newspapers. But no Katie.

"Where is she?" Nick muttered under his breath. "Katie, I'm here to help you. . . . Just shout if you can hear me."

He moved on to the next cabin. Turning the handle, Nick pushed against the door, but his effort was met with resistance. *There must be a leak on the other side,* he thought, giving the door a harder shove. It gave way under his strength, greeting Nick with a tide of stale-smelling water. Nick stepped into the room with trepidation.

"Katie? Are you here?" The beam settled on a black shelving unit with a small television set on it and a video camera on a tripod in the corner. The camera's lens was pointed toward a small couch.

Just as Nick was about to turn around and head out the door again, he felt something brushing against his leg. Startled, Nick spun around in the water, sucking in a frightened breath.

What he saw floating in the water behind him nearly made his heart explode.

"May I help you, young lady?"

Elizabeth smiled wanly at the chubby, dark-haired man who was sitting behind the desk at the tiny Coast Guard office. She had been standing there for nearly ten minutes, discreetly trying to get his attention, but the man was so engrossed in his meatball sub and fishing magazine that he didn't seem to even know she was there until he had reached the last bite.

"My sister rented a yacht yesterday, and it's urgent that I get in contact with her," Elizabeth said, staring at the radar panel and radio right behind him.

The man wiped his lips with a napkin and neatly scooped the crumbs off his desk as if he had absolutely all the time in the world. "When is your sister due back?"

"In a week."

He nodded slowly. "So she's not missing or anything?"

Elizabeth clenched the Jeep keys in her impatient fist. "No, she's not missing, but I think something might've happened to her," she said emphatically. "Please—let me radio her so at least I can find out if she's all right."

The man sighed and closed his magazine, then lumbered toward the counter. Elizabeth handed him a packet of papers with the details of the boat that she received from Pirate Perry's. He fished a pair of black-framed reading glasses out of the front pocket of his mint green dress shirt and examined the papers so thoroughly, it was as if he'd never seen them before. Elizabeth stared at him poker-faced, but her sneakered toes tapped with quietly impatient fury against the gray-tiled floor.

"Is your sister a good sailor?" he finally asked, looking up from the papers.

Elizabeth's brow furrowed. "No, but her companion is."

"That's good," the man said, taking off his reading glasses. "Because where they're headed, there's supposed to be a pretty severe thunderstorm within the next few hours. I hope they can handle it."

Great—as if I didn't have enough to worry about already, Elizabeth thought, feeling the tingle of anxiety creeping from the back of her neck down through her spine. She stared unflinchingly at the man. "I guess we'd better get on the radio right away, then," Elizabeth said with assertion, "so we can warn them about the storm."

Visibly defeated, the man grumbled inaudibly and made his way to the radio. Punching in the approximate coordinates on the radar panel, he sat back and waited a few seconds. Elizabeth leaned against the counter, hypnotized by the glowing, sweeping green arm of the radar.

"That's them," the man suddenly said, pointing a pudgy finger at one of the little green blips that showed up on the screen.

Elizabeth's toes stopped tapping and her muscles relaxed a bit. The feeling of helplessness was slipping away. She felt like she was finally taking concrete action to help her sister, even if she was nothing more than a tiny point of light on a screen.

The man turned a few dials and spoke into the silver microphone while Elizabeth watched the frequency needles bouncing with each word he spoke. "*Halcyon,* this is Coast Guard station number 391485—do you read?"

Elizabeth held her breath, waiting for the sound of a familiar voice to come over the radio. *Please, let everything be all right,* she thought. Her eyes burned with worry. *As soon as I speak to Jessica, I'll be able to sleep tonight.*

"*Halcyon* . . . do you read?" the man repeated.

Waking up from her daze, Elizabeth became acutely aware of the silence in the room.

"Maybe they're below deck and can't hear you," she ventured.

"There should be speakers in the cabin," he answered. Leaning over the microphone, the man radioed again, but there was still no answer.

Jessica—what has happened to you? Elizabeth's lungs forced her to take a quivering breath, and she quickly wiped away the hot tears that collected in the corners of her eyes. "They're not answering?"

The man shook his head. "I think the radio's dead. They probably unplugged it. Sometimes people on vacation like to do that, but we don't recommend it," he said. "I hope they at least had a chance to hear about the storm coming."

"Oh no." Elizabeth shook her head, wishing she could obliterate what she'd just heard. "Oh no. No. This is really bad—"

"You can try coming in tomorrow," he suggested blandly. "Maybe they'll plug the radio back in again."

"You don't understand. . . ." Elizabeth's voice trailed off as she started to lose control. The tears were rolling down her cheeks freely now, too fast for her to stop them. The man stared at her tear-stained face, his wet lips curved in slight amusement.

This is so humiliating, she thought. *Humiliating and horrible.* Elizabeth could've kicked herself right there and then—the last thing she wanted was for this unsympathetic man to see her crying. But if it would help him understand the urgency of the situation, she'd cry an entire ocean.

She took a deep breath and started again. "You don't understand. My sister is sailing with her boyfriend, and they were fighting, and . . . I have reason to believe that he may have hurt her."

The man smiled knowingly. "A lovers' quarrel, eh? I'm afraid there's not much we can do about that. We're only supposed to handle real emergencies."

"This *is* a real—" Elizabeth suddenly stopped short. *Why am I wasting my time here?* she thought suddenly. *I'm getting nowhere—this guy isn't going to help me.* Drying her tears, Elizabeth pulled her shoulders back and held her head high.

"Thank you for your time," Elizabeth said quietly. Turning on her heels, she headed out the door, her steps quickening to a sprint in a split second.

Chapter
Eight

"Now I know why Eric didn't want to come back here," Nick whispered in the inky darkness of the flooded cabin. A permanent chill seeped deep into his bones. Floating in the water right next to him was Katie's body, her face so battered and bruised that Nick could hardly imagine what she had looked like before the accident.

Nick's stomach lurched. He turned away from the body and vomited into the water. Then the shakes started, overtaking his entire body. Nick hadn't had the shakes since his first day on the force, when he still hadn't quite learned how to handle it.

You're losing it, Fox. Get a grip, he told himself, sucking in the oily air. *This is your job. You can't let it get to you.*

What got him was the dress. Katie was wearing the most beautiful floral sundress—the kind of thing any girl would buy for a special occasion to impress her boyfriend. As hard as he tried to push the morbid thoughts out of his mind, they kept resurfacing.

She had been having the time of her life and then— Nick felt his stomach lurch again. In his line of work the only dead bodies Nick was used to seeing were those of criminals who were mixed up in the dangerous drug trade or members of a crime family who were hit by one of their own. It was rare for Nick to see an innocent victim—and that only made seeing Katie even harder.

Nick covered Katie's body with the blanket he'd brought and said a silent prayer. "I guess I should head back now," he murmured under his breath, as if Katie could hear him. Somehow Nick felt almost guilty for leaving her in that dank, sinking compartment, but there was nothing else he could really do—Eric would freak out if he saw the body, and he certainly didn't want to traumatize Jessica. When the Coast Guard arrived, he'd send for her to be transported back to her family.

Nick waded through the water back to the sliver of light at the end of the cabin where the stairs were. He had moved past the galley, still unable to see the hole Eric was talking about, when Nick suddenly paused.

The refrigerator . . .

Nick's eyes narrowed in confusion. Eric had said that the refrigerator had toppled over and crushed Katie—he was sure of it. He went over the conversation again in his mind, wondering—*hoping*—he had been mistaken because right there in front of him was the refrigerator.

It was standing upright.

I'm sure that's what he said, Nick told himself. *I pictured it all so clearly in my head.* But if Katie had been pinned underneath anything—forget about the refrigerator—so tightly that even Eric couldn't have saved her, how could the body have gotten loose?

There's something very, very wrong about all of this, Nick thought, no longer able to ignore the gnawing suspicions that kept building in his head. Nick sailed up the stairs, taking them two at a time, his eyes squinting as they adjusted to the light. When he got back, Eric would have a lot of explaining to do.

With quick fingers Nick untied the rope that held the aluminum boat. A strange urgency was building inside him like the darkening clouds that were beginning to envelop the sun. Nick had never been superstitious, but he couldn't help thinking that the approaching storm was a sign—an omen of some kind.

"I'll be back soon, Jess," he promised aloud, hoping that somehow she could hear him. "I'm on my way right now."

But just as Nick was about to leave the sinking schooner, he looked out across the rough waves at the yacht. He froze, rope in hand. The *Halcyon* had been completely turned around and was speeding out of sight.

"Come back!" Nick cried. He fell to his knees on the tilted deck, his arms outstretched in despair. But it was no use—they were leaving him behind, with only a dead body as consolation.

Jessica's head felt fuzzy, as if it had been stuffed with cotton. Slowly, with an enormous struggle, she was becoming lucid, trying to comprehend her surroundings. With her eyes still shut, she didn't know what to make of the cool, wet surface pressing against the side of her face or the continuous rising and falling of whatever it was that she was on. Most confusing of all were the screeching sounds of an electric guitar that assaulted her groggy ears.

What's going on? Jessica wondered, opening her eyes to a gauzy fog. *Where am I, at a frat party or something?*

Daylight pierced the haze, making her head ache terribly. No. This was *definitely* not a party.

As her eyes adjusted, Jessica became aware of a rising and falling strip of blue that kept entering and disappearing from her line of vision. *Ocean,* her brain said. *Boat . . . you're on a boat.* The clues kept coming, one by one, until Jessica was able to complete the picture of what had happened over the last few hours. A resurging fear pulsed through Jessica's veins as she remembered how Nick left her alone with Eric, the lunatic, to check out the sinking boat. She remembered the smack of his hand across her face.

She wished she had never woken up.

"Have a good nap?" Eric called to her from across the deck, bouncing wildly to the music on Nick's portable, waterproof radio.

Jessica didn't answer. Instead she rubbed her sore head and suppressed the urge to cry. As her vision cleared she saw Eric staring at her with a lecherous grin on his face while his hips swayed to the beat. Jessica looked away, her stomach turning. *This creep is really out of his mind,* she thought, hugging her shaking knees to her chest in a self-protective gesture. *When is Nick going to get here?*

"Stop sitting there like a grouch," Eric said, snapping his fingers and licking his lips. "Come on! This is our own private party!"

Not if I can help it, Jessica thought, gritting her teeth. With each moment that passed, her thoughts became sharper and her terror was heightened. Jessica rose to her knees and discreetly glimpsed out on the water to see how close Nick was to returning. He was nowhere in sight.

Neither was the other boat.

Jessica stifled a cry. Without thinking, she bolted to her feet and stared out at the water, searching for some remnant of the sinking ship, but there was none.

It can't be gone, she told herself, her body paralyzed with white-hot alarm. *Where's Nick? Please tell me he didn't go down with the boat—*

"Are you looking for your bad-boy detective?" Eric shouted, his black eyes smoldering like coals.

A lightening bolt of fury nearly split Jessica in two. *If anything has happened to him, Eric, I swear I'll kill you,* she vowed silently. She fought to maintain an icy, detached exterior despite the turmoil that was tearing her insides apart. The last thing she wanted was to get Eric riled up and have him attack her again. She had to be careful, calculating.

"What did you do with Nick?" Jessica asked almost offhandedly, as if she were inquiring about the finer points of sailing, all the while trying to ignore the raging inferno in her heart. "Didn't he come back yet?"

Eric raised his strong arms in the air and swung his hips in circles, as if he were playing with an invisible Hula Hoop. "Nick's still on the schooner."

Jessica's mouth went dry. Her knees seemed to buckle beneath her, so she reached weakly for the railing to steady herself.

"Watch it there," Eric said, studying her closely. "You wouldn't want to fall again."

"Rough seas," Jessica answered numbly. *My sweet Nick . . . if only you had listened to me. . . . Why did you have to play the hero?* With trembling fingers Jessica smoothed back her hair. Even though her reason for living was nowhere to be seen, she couldn't break down—not yet. Her own survival was at stake.

"So we're alone now," Jessica breathed casually, forcing a sweet smile on her face. There was a rough question she had to ask—a bile-churning, revolting question—but it was the only one she could think of that had a snowball's chance of getting the truth out of her captor. "I can't believe that the schooner went down so quick, Eric. I wish I could've been awake to see it. Was it cool?"

Eric dropped his arms at his sides. His forehead wrinkled as if he were slightly confused.

"The schooner didn't go down, not yet anyway," he said. "I just turned the engine on and drove the boat away."

The numbness and anger suddenly lifted from Jessica's quaking frame, replaced by an exuberant, joyous hope. *Nick is still alive—he has to be!* she cheered silently. *All I have to do is get back to him.* Her spirits and strength renewed, Jessica bounded across the deck and reached for the steering wheel.

Eric turned off the radio. "What are you doing?"

Think of something quick, urged a voice inside Jessica's head. *Don't let him get suspicious.*

"We have to go back," she blurted.

"What do you mean?"

"I . . . I've never seen a boat sink before," Jessica said, making a quick save. "I thought it would be cool to watch."

Eric reached in front of her and clicked off the engine. "It's not that big a deal, really." He stared at her through hooded eyelids, a seductive smile playing on his lips. "Besides, I thought it might be a lot nicer if the two of us had a little time alone."

It was all too clear what it was going to take to get her way. If she wanted to save Nick, she was going to have to play nice with Eric. *Really* nice.

Eric hovered over her, his mouth hanging

open like a hungry dog's. Jessica bit her lower lip in an attempt to quell the wrenching sensation in her stomach, but judging from the sudden grin on Eric's face, he actually believed she was flirting with him. *Please forgive me for what I'm about to do, Nick, but there's no other choice. . . .*

Jessica pressed herself against him forcefully and looked deeply into Eric's maniacal eyes. What she found there was disgusting and horrifying, but she knew she had to tamp down her nausea—for Nick's sake. "Spending time alone with you, Eric?" she answered huskily. "There's nothing else I'd rather do."

Jessica's touch sent a searing fire coursing through Eric's veins. He stared at her for a moment in disbelief. *Am I dreaming this or is it real?* he wondered. *How often in someone's life does their greatest fantasy come true?*

Eric slipped his arms around Jessica's trim waist and watched her reaction, but she didn't flinch. To the contrary, she seemed exceptionally pleased. "Are you serious, or are you just playing with me?"

Her startlingly blue eyes looked down shyly as she traced circles with her fingertips on his chest. "I can't believe you'd ask me such a question, Eric."

"You locked me in that room," Eric said,

distracted by her silky touch. "I thought you hated me."

Jessica's blond hair shifted direction with the strong wind, blowing golden strands across her tanned face. Gently he brushed the hair out of her eyes, his body nearly melting from the joy of it.

"That was a big misunderstanding, Eric." Jessica's bright smile suddenly turned into a frown. "I didn't want to do it. It was all Nick's idea. He can be really jealous sometimes."

"But why didn't you let me out when I hollered to you?"

A sly glimmer sparkled in Jessica's eyes. "I thought it might be fun to see how strong you really are." As Jessica said this she squeezed his biceps, her tingling touch still burning the surface of his skin long after she was done. "And soon enough I found out for myself . . . ," she said, rubbing the purple bruise that was swelling near her right temple.

Eric's smiling face dissolved into a severe look. "I'm sorry about that, Jessica. I have a really bad temper—it's better if you don't play around too much because I can really fly off the handle, and we don't want that to happen. Not when we're having so much fun."

Jessica nodded earnestly, as if she knew she had been in the wrong and had deserved what she got. The gesture made his chest swell with joy.

She's absolutely perfect, Eric thought, relief flooding his senses and giving him a renewed energy. *Finally I've found a woman who can un-derstand me.* His head spun, overwhelmed by the sudden surge of love that was pounding in his heart. Smiling with glee, he held Jessica close. *I can't believe this. I think I've found my soul mate. . . .*

"I'm so glad we're together, Eric," Jessica murmured sensuously, echoing his sentiments. "I almost feel like we were meant for each other."

"Me too," he whispered breathlessly in Jessica's ear. His heart was so full, he thought it might burst. *I never imagined love could be like this. . . .*

Carried away on the wave of emotion, Eric leaned toward Jessica, his eyes closed, his lips aching to be touched by hers. He needed her so badly, it was almost painful. As he moved closer he felt her breath on his skin. He drank in the delicious agony of the moment, never wanting it to end and at the same time longing for the in-evitable embrace. Closer . . . closer . . . and just as their lips almost touched, Jessica pulled away.

"What . . . ?" Eric glanced down at his empty arms, his lips on fire.

Jessica was walking away, tossing him a flirty look over her shoulder. Her face was flushed. "I thought maybe I'd get us both something to drink," she said. "I'm feeling a bit warm—aren't you?"

Eric nodded wordlessly, watching her walk toward the stairs. *So she likes to play hard to get,* he thought, his bare chest heaving. *This is going to be even more fun than I imagined!*

"Jessica!" Nick shouted futilely into the wind, the yacht nearly a pinpoint on the horizon.

What is going on? he wondered in shock. Did Eric get loose and take over? Or is Jessica behind the wheel, intending to get closer to the schooner and doing a totally rotten job of trying to control the boat?

Nick tended to believe the latter, remembering how Jessica rolled her eyes every time he tried to teach her how to handle the yacht. Nick's stomach clenched in frustration. "None of this would be happening if you had paid a little attention!" he yelled into the pounding surf.

As he glared angrily at the ocean Nick noticed a marked difference in the water level from when he first arrived. The side rails of the schooner were now starting to submerge—yes, the boat was definitely sinking.

There's no point in being mad at Jessica now, whispered a calm voice in his mind. *It's not going to help you get out of the situation.* Time was running out. He'd have to work fast.

Nick weighed his options. He could patiently wait to see if Jessica would turn around and come back for him, or he could jump into the rowboat and try to catch up. There was virtually no chance he'd have the strength to row after the yacht, which was not out of his line of sight, let alone catch up to it. But looking up at the darkening sky and rough seas, Nick knew that the schooner wouldn't last too long either. Nick shuddered. If Jessica couldn't control the yacht now, what was she going to do when the storm hit?

Then he suddenly had an idea. *The radio . . . I'll fix the radio and call her. I'll tell her what to do, and she can come back for me before the weather goes bad.* Nick slapped his knee. It was the perfect solution.

"Except for one thing." Nick sighed, the problem dawning on him the second he hit the stairs. "There's no electricity to power the radio."

If he was lucky, the schooner would have a gas-run generator, as most boats that size did. Nick lowered himself into the bleak, dark hole he had hoped never to see again and sloshed through the dungeonlike cabin toward the engine room. He opened the door and slipped inside quickly, hoping to keep as much water out of the room as possible. Sitting there, as if by some miracle, was the generator Nick had been hoping to find.

"Thank goodness *something* is going right today," Nick said aloud, kneeling on the damp floor. The generator was full of gasoline. Nick clasped his hands thankfully.

Bracing one foot against the generator, Nick grasped the handle and gave the cord a good, hard tug. It took several tries, but soon the generator was running, illuminating even a dim bulb in the engine room. Nick exhaled loudly, allowing himself to smile for the first time in hours.

Tiredly Nick pushed the door open again and walked through the water, which had nearly risen to his hips. The galley seemed much less intimidating now that there was light. The cupboards were all hanging open from the odd angle of the boat, their contents spilled out into the water. For the first time he could see the hole below the stove where the propane tank had exploded.

Nick spotted the radio at the other end, near the cabin where he had found Katie. As he waded closer Nick swore he heard the faint sound of voices coming from behind the door where Katie was. *You're hallucinating, Fox. No one's here,* he told himself. *No one alive anyway.* But the more he tried to talk himself out of it, the louder the voices became.

"Who's in here?" he shouted as toughly as he could, but still the voices chattered on as if they didn't hear him. "I am a police officer! Tell me who you are . . . now!"

Backing against the door of the cabin, Nick listened in to hear what they were saying, his body poised for action. "Wait a minute," he murmured, starting to laugh out loud. He had nearly forgotten there was a television set inside the cabin. It must've been left on before the power shut off. Nick pushed open the door and leaned limply in the doorway, his nerves exhausted and frazzled.

"Just the TV," he murmured to himself, looking up on the screen. It looked like a home movie or something, with bad lighting and sound. The tape showed a woman sitting on the couch looking at the camera. She was wearing a pretty floral sundress. *That must be Katie,* Nick thought sadly. He walked into the cabin, drawn to the screen by curiosity, and stared at the woman. Her face was obscured by shadows, and she wasn't saying anything. But even the shadows couldn't hide her eyes. They stared blankly, looking haunted and lost.

"Say something," said the voice off camera—it sounded like Eric. He seemed to be impatient with her. She didn't respond. Nick was suddenly confused. They hardly seemed to be in love at all.

Why do those eyes look so familiar? Nick thought, moving closer and closer to the television. Katie's body had been unrecognizable, but those eyes—he had to have seen her somewhere before. But where? Nick tried to see through the shadows surrounding those dark, puffy eyes and their tired, weather-beaten expression to jog his memory.

"State your name," Eric's voice said harshly.

Then the answer came to him in a horrifying flash. Nick stared at the screen in stunned recognition as he and the woman said the name in unison.

"Katherine Horstmueller."

Chapter Nine

Katherine Horstmueller . . .

Katie.

It was the woman Nick had been trying to rescue from the kidnapper before everything had gone so wrong. Nick glanced at the blanket-covered body, his chest feeling as if it were collapsing on itself. *She's dead,* he thought, the realization ricocheting around his brain like a firing squad's bullets. *I can't believe she's dead. . . .*

"Please tell the folks at home why you're here," Eric joked from behind the camera, as if he were the emcee of a game show.

Oh no, this can't mean . . .

Nick tried to breathe, but his lungs refused to fill with air.

Eric is . . .

Eric is . . .

"I have been kidnapped. . . ."

"That's good, darling, that's really good," Eric's voice said with manic energy. "Now why don't you explain the rules of the game to those at home who haven't played before."

The camera zoomed in for a close-up, and Katherine's huge, frightened eyes engulfed the screen, the shadows falling away to reveal blank terror all over her young, beautiful face. She opened her quivering mouth as if to speak, but no sound escaped.

"Come *on*, sweetheart, you were doing so well," Eric coaxed. His voice had an impatient edge. "Tell your mommy and daddy all about the money we want and what's going to happen to you if we don't get it."

Katherine didn't speak.

Say something, Nick pleaded silently, as if it could somehow change what was about to happen.

The camera pulled back sharply, and Katherine's face disappeared into shadows once again. "Tell them, Katherine."

The young woman moved suddenly, her eyes looking away. "I'm not going to do it."

"You *will* do it."

Don't fight him, Katherine, Nick pleaded. *Just do whatever he asks. . . .*

"No. I'm not going to do it."

Suddenly Eric appeared on-screen. He yanked Katherine by the hair and pulled her head back to look him in the face. "Say it!" Eric's voice sounded as if it was hissed through gritted teeth.

Katherine didn't answer.

Say it. Tears welled in the corners of Nick's eyes. He couldn't stand the thought of what was about to happen next, and yet he couldn't bring himself to look away.

"I hope you never see one dime of my parents' money," Katherine said dully. Then she spit in Eric's face.

No, Katherine. Oh no . . .

The humiliation was obvious in Eric's eyes. He let go of Katherine's hair and took two steps away from her. Then every line of his face took on an edge as hard as steel and his teeth bared like a rabid dog's. The transformation was so unrelentingly evil that it made Nick's blood turn to ice. Worst of all was the look in Eric's eyes—a vicious, almost gleeful stare that knew no limits and had no conscience.

Nick watched in horror as Eric drew back his arm and struck a powerful blow to Katherine's head.

"No!" Nick yelled, dashing out of the room. He couldn't watch the rest. Crushing guilt bore down on him like a two-ton granite boulder.

"Katherine Horstmueller is dead, and it's all my fault," he cried aloud, covering his stinging eyes in shame with his hands. "I could've saved her and I blew it."

Taking the hostage out on the water was a stroke of genius—no one in the department would have thought to look for the kidnapper there. Then suddenly the pieces fell into place. It all seemed so brutally clear.

Eric must have known who I was all along. He's been playing a game. I was after him . . .

. . . and now he's after me.

And if there was one way that Eric could completely and permanently destroy Nick, it would be to take Jessica away from him.

Nick sank to his knees in the sinking schooner's murky water.

"No, not Jessica!" he cried out from the depths of his soul. "Please, don't let Jessica be next!"

"I hope you like lemonade!" Jessica called over her shoulder as she descended the stairs to the galley.

"Sounds great, darling," Eric answered, taking over the steering wheel. "Make mine real sweet." He let out a loud, bellowing laugh—the kind that made Jessica's skin crawl. As if her skin wasn't crawling enough already.

120

"I'll be right back." Jessica's heart slammed against her rib cage sickeningly. She pressed her fingers to her lips, cringing as she thought of the kiss she'd narrowly escaped. She could still feel Eric's eager hands all over her, burning into her skin like acid.

That was close . . . too close, Jessica thought, her stomach churning. *At least I held him off for a while.*

But how long could she keep it up?

Jessica braced herself against the handrail at the bottom of the stairs, fighting against a sudden swell that was bucking and rocking the yacht. She nearly burst into tears thinking about Nick, out there all alone on the sinking schooner, with no means of escape but a flimsy metal boat. Did he think she intentionally abandoned him? Or did he have the sense to realize that Eric was behind it all?

One thing was certain: She had to figure out a way to get the yacht back to Nick. Frantic thoughts sparked in Jessica's mind as she tried to formulate a plan. There was certainly no convincing Eric to turn around, at least not without making him very suspicious. And the way he was breathing down her neck almost every second, there was virtually no chance for her to take control of the boat herself.

The only way I can get control of the situation

121

is to get Eric out of the way, Jessica realized, trying to swallow the hard lump that seemed lodged in her throat. It seemed awfully drastic, but she'd do anything to save Nick, not to mention avoid the lip locking with Eric that lay on the horizon like certain doom.

"Think fast," Jessica whispered under her breath as she stumbled across the moving floor. "He's going to be down here any minute." Quickly and methodically she worked her way through the kitchen cabinets and then over to the storage drawers underneath the booth in the dining area. Drawer after drawer, there was nothing but food and household items, a medicine kit someone must've left behind from the last charter, and a few board games. There wasn't even a sharp knife to threaten Eric with.

This is not good, Jessica thought grimly. *My only options are either to knock him out with a can of beef stew or to bore him into a coma with a backgammon tournament.* But neither solution seemed very effective.

Eric's footsteps sounded a terrifying warning above Jessica's head. *Oh no, here he comes!* Jessica jumped to her feet. An excruciating pressure was building in her temples like a volcano that was about to erupt. *Where else can I look?*

A moment later her darting eyes came to rest on the closet near the bathroom where Nick had found his supplies before he left to go on the schooner. *This is it—there has to be something I can use in here.* Opening the door with anxious fingers, Jessica reached into the dark closet. Her searching hands felt along the edges of cardboard boxes of rope and emergency flares, plastic rain suits, and Nick's fishing equipment. Feeling along the wall, her fingers at last found a long, cool object that felt like the barrel of a gun.

Jessica's jaw fell open slightly in disbelief. Did she even dare to hope? Carefully she reached in and pulled out the slender neck of a dart gun.

This will do quite nicely, Jessica thought, turning the gun over in her trembling hands. In her mind she pictured herself storming up the stairs, taking Eric by surprise. She'd threaten him with the gun, tie him up with the few spare lengths of rope, then turn the boat around to go after Nick.

A bubble of hope rose in the middle of Jessica's chest. *It's the perfect plan,* she thought, releasing the safety lock. *Hang on, Nick, I'm coming for you. . . .*

"Jessica!" Eric called from the deck.

Clasping her hand over her mouth to stifle her frightened cries, Jessica froze, dropping the box of cartridges at her feet. She didn't even dare to breathe.

"What?" Jessica answered as evenly as she could. The sound of her heartbeat boomed in her ears like a bass drum.

Eric's shadow loomed above the stairs. "I just wanted to see what was taking so long down here." The red, sunburned tops of his feet appeared as he began to descend the stairs.

Horrified, Jessica looked down at the gun in her hands and the scattered dart cartridges at her feet. Everything happened so slowly, as if it were in a dream. Jessica seemed to be watching herself from a distance as she tossed the dart gun into the closet, then kicked the cartridges in with it. She dashed toward the kitchen counter and opened the cupboard door where the dishes were kept with a second to spare.

"I was getting kind of thirsty up there," Eric said, watching her with smoldering eyes.

Thank goodness he didn't catch me, Jessica thought. She gave Eric an honestly bright smile, enjoying the fact that he had absolutely no idea why she was genuinely happy at that moment. "Sorry, I'm still feeling a little dizzy," she said, holding her head. "Oooh, ouch."

Eric pouted his lips. "Next time you'll know that you should do what I say," he said ominously, his dark eyes intense. "You should *always* do what I say."

The smile quickly faded from Jessica's face. "Of course. Whatever you say."

"Good." Eric's mouth broke into a huge smile, his teeth glowing white against his sunburned face. He tore his eyes away from Jessica for a moment and looked at the bare countertop. "Where's the lemonade?"

Lemonade . . . lemonade . . . Jessica had been so absorbed with working out a plan to get Nick that she'd totally forgotten about it. She looked down at the empty counter, feeling the heat of Eric's stare on the back of her neck. *He's going to know I was up to something.*

"You know, I'm *really* embarrassed about this." Jessica spun around and faced Eric, leaning back casually on her elbows. "Here I go and offer you fresh lemonade, and we don't even have lemons." Jessica pulled all the stops—a girlish, sly wink, a flirtatious toss of the hair—anything so she could keep Eric's trust.

Eric shrugged, then grabbed Jessica's upper arm roughly, as if she were a piece of property. "It's no big deal. Let's go up on deck and pick up where we left off."

"No, really," Jessica stammered, gently trying to pull herself away from his iron grip. "I promised I'd make you a drink. How about some iced tea?"

125

"I don't really care—"

"I insist," Jessica replied assertively. She moved a little closer to him despite the rising nausea in the pit of her stomach and traced the contours of Eric's collarbone with her fingers. "I want to make you something, Eric. Please let me do something nice for you."

Eric closed his eyes, looking as if he were melting away like the Wicked Witch of the West. "All right," Eric breathed. He suddenly wrapped his arms around Jessica and pulled her crushingly close. She could feel his lips tracing the edge of her ear. "When you're all done, then you can let *me* do some nice things for *you*."

Jessica stiffened. Judging from Eric's sexy tone, he wasn't talking about making lemonade. "Sounds perfect." She sighed against his shoulder, trying desperately not to gag.

Eric's hands started moving up and down her back. "You drive me crazy, Jessica."

"Mmmm. Now *that's* what I like in a man." Jessica pushed him away playfully. "Later!"

Eric groaned as if releasing her was more painful than a root canal. "I'll be waiting for you up on deck." He winked, turned, and headed toward the stairs.

"I won't be long this time." Jessica blew a kiss at Eric's retreating back. That was when she noticed that the closet door was still open.

If he sees the dart gun, I'm dead. Drops of perspiration beaded her forehead. Eric was only a foot away from the closet; in fact, it looked as if he was heading right for it. *Please don't notice . . . please.*

It was the only hope she had left.

Chapter Ten

"I think I feel a squall coming," Jessica told Eric. "Maybe you should take down the sails."

Eric stopped and turned around. He loved the way she was constantly worrying about every little detail. "It's not a problem. I love sailing in rough weather."

"Whatever you say, Eric," Jessica answered, taking two glasses down from the cupboard. "I'm sure you know what's best."

She trusts me, he thought with a happy sigh. Eric had started to head up the stairs when he noticed the open closet door. Through the opening he could see that it was a mess inside, boxes overturned, their contents spilling out. It looked as though someone had been tearing through it, searching for something. In a big hurry.

"Did you go into the closet?" Eric asked, his eyes narrowing in suspicion.

Jessica, who was busy filling the cups with ice, kept her back to him. "No, why do you ask?"

Eric kicked open the door. Propped against the inside of the closet was a dart gun with cartridges scattered all over the floor.

Jessica took a box of tea bags from the cupboard, humming contentedly to herself as if she had no idea what he was doing. She wouldn't even look at him. "I hope iced tea is OK—it's all we have." She giggled. "It seems like all I've made for you is tea, Eric. I promise tonight to make you something really special."

Eric's thick fingers wrapped around the barrel of the gun, and he pulled it out of the closet. *The safety catch is released,* he realized, examining the gun. *It looks like someone tried to load it.* He stood there, silent, the gun hanging by his side, staring at the back of Jessica's pretty blond head as she scurried around making tea, all sweetness and innocence, acting as if nothing was wrong.

A burning red anger seared Eric's torso at her deception. It quickly spread through his limbs like wildfire. *You'd better not have any cute tricks up your sleeve, Jessica,* he seethed. *Because I'll be your worst nightmare.*

"You're not lying to me, are you?" Eric hissed through gritted teeth. He loaded a cartridge and raised the gun. "Think long and hard before you answer, Jessica."

Jessica spooned sugar into the cups. Long blond strands of hair covered her face. "What are you talking about, the closet?"

The cool metal barrel itched in Eric's palms. "You were going through it, weren't you? When you said you were making lemonade? You were trying to pull something over on me, sweetheart, am I right?"

"No way, Eric," Jessica answered calmly, stirring the tea. "Why would I do that? I *want* to be with you. The last person who was in the closet was Nick, right before he went to the schooner. He brought some supplies with him. If it's a mess in there, it's his fault." Jessica paused a moment and shook her head, her face still out of view. "If there's one thing that I absolutely can't stand about the guy, it's the messes he leaves everywhere. Me, I'm a total neatnik. I'm always cleaning up, you know?"

Eric lowered the gun. Jessica's words were like a misty rain diffusing his fiery anger. He wanted so much to believe her, but he still wasn't completely convinced that she was telling the truth. *Look in her eyes,* he thought. *Then you'll know.*

"Look at me, Jessica," Eric ordered.

Jessica dropped the spoon into the sink and slowly turned around. She brushed her hair back out of her face and looked up at him. Then her beautiful blue eyes widened in horror.

"What's that?" she cried, pointing to the dart gun. "Please, Eric, don't point that thing at me!"

Eric couldn't help laughing in spite of himself. "It's a dart gun, Jess. Don't worry about it," he said. "You've never seen one of these before?"

Jessica shook her head nervously. "That was in the closet?"

She's too surprised to be making this up, Eric decided, feeling the fire subside. He smiled at her. *I'm so glad you weren't lying to me, Jessica. I was right—you really are the woman for me. Now that Fox is out of the picture, we're going to be so happy together. I promise.*

A warm glow of contentment swept over Eric and left a giddy smile on his face. This had to be the happiest day of his life. Not only had he managed to expertly knock off Nick Fox, the only detective who had ever come close to capturing him, but he had also managed to get his girl. It was the perfect revenge.

Eric dropped the gun by his side and finished loading the chamber with cartridges. "This is a handy piece of equipment," he said, showing off his firearms expertise for Jessica's benefit. He flexed his pecs to give her the whole macho nine yards. "You shouldn't be afraid of it."

"I hate guns." Jessica backed away, trembling. "Please put it away."

Eric strapped the gun to his bare back and headed for the stairs to the deck. "I'd better keep it close by, Jess," Eric said, flashing her a bright smile. "You never know who might drop in."

As he climbed the stairs he told himself, *No one can touch me. Especially not Nick Fox—not anymore. I'm invincible.*

"If the Coast Guard doesn't care, then who will?" Elizabeth muttered to herself. She shoved her hands into the pockets of her red Windbreaker and went down to the docks. Late afternoon clouds were beginning to roll in, and the temperature was starting to drop. Soon night would fall, making any kind of search for the boat nearly impossible. Elizabeth zipped up her jacket and paced the splintered wood of the dock, trying to push down the swell of hysteria that was rising in her chest.

Stay cool, she told herself. *Think things through.*

Elizabeth reached the end of the dock and

stared out at the gray-blue water. The chilling sea breeze loosened wisps of golden hair from her long braid, softly framing her face. "It wouldn't do any good to go to the police," she said aloud, turning around and retracing her steps. "They'd think I was nuts if I told them Nick hurt Jessica."

"Excuse me," called a deep, resonant voice from behind her. "Is there something I can help you with?"

Elizabeth spun on her heels and turned her head in the direction of the voice, but she didn't see anyone.

"I'm over here," the voice came again.

A waving hand brought her attention to a sleek, midnight blue racer with silver detailing anchored to the dock. The owner of the boat stuck his head out from behind the jib, his deep blue eyes nearly matching the sparkling paint on his boat. "You look a little lost."

"I'm—no, I'm not lost." Elizabeth was flustered by the way the young man's sandy, wind-blown hair fell seductively across his gorgeous, olive-complected, chiseled face.

"Um, my sister's out there. . . ." Elizabeth trailed off, her cheeks warming with embarrassment.

"There's a pretty big storm coming," he answered with a strong note of concern. "I was just out there myself for about an hour and decided to come back. It's getting pretty rough."

The corners of Elizabeth's mouth turned down. "The weather is the least of my worries right now."

The gorgeous stranger dropped the jib sheet he was holding and stared at her with such honest intensity that Elizabeth had to look away. "What's wrong?"

He seemed like a nice enough guy, but Elizabeth decided it wouldn't be right to dump her troubles on him. "Thanks for asking, but I really don't want to burden you." Elizabeth smiled politely, then started walking away.

"No, wait—" he called after her. "Please tell me. If there's any way I can help . . ."

Elizabeth paused for a beat or two, then turned around and headed back toward the boat. "My sister, Jessica, is sailing out there with her boyfriend, and I'm almost positive she's in trouble—big trouble."

"What kind of trouble?"

Elizabeth hesitated, remembering the reaction of the man at the Coast Guard office. "I'd really rather not say—other than I think she might be in some sort of physical danger."

The stranger's brow creased as he stepped over the rigging of his racer and sat down on the bow. He was much taller than Elizabeth had originally thought. "You should contact the Coast Guard," he said, pointing at the north side of the marina. "There's an office—"

"I know," Elizabeth interrupted. "I tried to radio her from there, but there was no response. The man at the office told me they probably just disconnected their radio because they're on vacation and that I should try again tomorrow."

"That's the most absurd thing I've ever heard. It's more likely that the radio's down."

Elizabeth nodded, feeling some of the burden lifting from her shoulders. *Maybe Nick wouldn't do something that foolish after all*, she thought, relieved to finally find a person who was at least willing to listen to her problem.

"So you don't think someone would disconnect their radio on purpose?" Elizabeth asked.

The stranger ran his fingers through his long bangs. "They'd have to be crazy to do something like that, especially with a storm on the way."

Maybe there's nothing wrong at all, Elizabeth suddenly hoped. *Maybe it's just another one of Jessica's dramatic performances, and I've blown it way out of proportion*. But there had been a scream and a splash—and the phone call Jessica made, crying hysterically. How could Elizabeth have misinterpreted all those things? An unexpected wave of emotion

136

swept over her, tormenting her with the impending threat of tears.

"I just don't know what to do," she said quietly.

"If you want to try calling her again, I have a radio you can use," he offered.

Elizabeth nearly jumped at the opportunity, but a nagging voice in the corner of her brain held her back. *Are you crazy?* it said. *You don't even know this guy. He could be a psychopath.* Elizabeth ignored the voice and stared deeply into the stranger's twinkling blue eyes. *Psychopath or not,* she decided, *he's the best chance I've got.*

"Thank you—so much. I really appreciate it," Elizabeth said, extending her hand to him. "My name is Elizabeth Wakefield."

He smiled warmly. "It's nice to meet you, Elizabeth," he answered, taking her hand. "I'm Matt Birch. Now come on in. Let's find out what's up with your sister."

"Jessica, this is Nick. Do you read me?" Nick waited for a moment, but still there was no answer. He turned a few dials on the radio instrument panel and tried again. "Jessica, if you hear me, pick up the handset."

Still nothing.

Pounding his frustrated fists against the

panel, Nick realized it was a lost cause. He wasn't altogether surprised that the radio was in perfect working condition despite Eric's statements to the contrary; nothing could really surprise him now. But his inability to get through to Jessica was another matter.

"I just don't get it. The radio was working fine when I left." He ran his fingers anxiously through his hair, trying to contemplate his next move, but all he could see in his mind was Jessica lying bound and gagged on the deck of the yacht at the mercy of a madman. The broom handle had been a dumb idea. Seeing Eric's violent strength on the videotape made Nick realize that if Eric really wanted to get out of the locked cabin, there was nothing that could hold him back. There was nothing at all to stop him.

That probably explains what happened to the radio. The thought made Nick shiver uncontrollably. Maybe Jessica had heard Eric pounding on the door, trying to escape, and had tried to use the radio to call the schooner. *When Eric finally broke loose, he found her calling for help and smashed the radio or disconnected it or something.* He could see it all in his mind as clearly as what he had just seen on the television in the cabin.

Nick covered his swollen, exhausted face

with his hands. He didn't have the strength to even think about what could've happened next. *Whatever happens, Jessica, do what he says,* he pleaded as if Jessica could receive his message telepathically. *Don't try to fight him. You can't win.*

"It's so cold in here," Nick grumbled, suddenly realizing that his voice was no longer echoing throughout the schooner. The seawater had risen a good three or four inches since he'd arrived. The frigid, salty water had seemed to find its way into every tiny gap and opening of Nick's orange rain suit and boots, slowly and steadily drenching his jeans and shirt underneath. His skin was starting to lose some of its sensation in the low temperature, feeling numb and thick as though it were made of rubber. Aware of the danger of hypothermia, Nick jumped around in the water a bit to get the blood flowing and forced his eyes wide open to ward off any drowsiness.

"Go up on deck for a while, Fox, and warm up." Nick shouted at himself to stay alert. But when he reached the deck, there were no balmy breezes or shining rays of sun to warm him. The sky was covered with thick, black storm clouds that grew darker and more ominous toward the horizon. The seas were higher, running four to six feet, and the foamy white crests crashed against the tilted deck. Nick's foot slipped on the wet deck, but the mast broke his fall, stopping him from sliding into the sea.

"You can't do this to me!" Nick shouted furiously, shaking his fists at the stormy sky. His heart dropped to the ocean floor when he saw the aluminum boat he had rowed in on floating away. It had broken free of its rope and was being carried away by the tossing waves. There was no escape from the sinking ship.

A crack of thunder sounded, and without mercy the rains came, pelting Nick like cold nails. It was as if all the forces of nature were conspiring to keep him and Jessica apart.

"Whatever happens, Jessica, know that I will always love you," Nick whispered to the churning sea, hoping the waves would carry the message to the one he loved.

Chapter Eleven

Oh, Nick, what is happening to you out there?
Jessica wondered silently as she stared out the porthole window in the kitchen at the frightening storm clouds that had closed in, pouring down rain that sounded unrelenting. She had been one precious, tantalizing step closer to being able to go back and save her boyfriend, but that was before Eric found the gun. Now that he was walking around with it strapped to his back like a commando, there was no chance of getting it back.

"This is a total nightmare," Jessica whispered under her breath. Tears beaded her lashes, threatening to explode into a deluge. "No matter how crazy he is, he won't stay up on deck too long in this rain." She slumped tiredly against the counter, feeling as if her body had been completely drained of its lifeblood. *I don't know if I can keep this up,* Jessica thought. *I don't know if I can go on.*

A surging wave crashed against the side of the boat, shaking Jessica out of her stupor and nearly knocking over the glasses of iced tea she had made. She breathed deeply and dried her eyes, her mind regaining its focus. "I have to be strong," she told herself. "I have to do this for Nick."

It was at that very moment, when Jessica thought all hope was lost, that the idea came to her. She didn't know if it would work, but it was definitely worth a try.

First Jessica checked the stairs to see if Eric was coming, and when the coast was clear, she dove for the storage drawer underneath the dining booth. There it was, in the second drawer, right next to the deck of cards, exactly where she remembered seeing it.

Jessica opened the lid to the medicine kit and looked inside. Mingled with the cotton swabs, Ace bandages, and tubes of ointment were packets of aspirin, a few over-the-counter painkillers, and some cold remedies. But when Jessica pushed aside the metal box of Band-Aids, underneath she found the treasure she was hoping for: a brown prescription bottle filled with sleeping pills. "Take one to two capsules

142

before bedtime. Do not exceed maximum dosage of six pills within a twenty-four-hour period," Jessica read from the label.

Perfect, she thought, snagging eight of the red-and-yellow capsules. *This is exactly what I need.*

Careful to close the drawer properly—she didn't want to make the same mistake she had made with the supply closet—Jessica rushed over to the counter and started cracking the capsules open, pouring the white powder into one of the iced tea cups.

Three . . . four . . . five . . .

The dosage was a little high, but it certainly couldn't be enough to kill him. Besides, she needed a guarantee that Eric wouldn't wake up until Nick was safely on board again.

Six . . . seven . . . eight . . .

The white powder floated down through the iced tea like flakes of snow in a dome paperweight and collected in a thick layer at the bottom of the cup. This stuff looked as if it would never dissolve. Jessica grabbed a spoon from the sink and stirred the iced tea furiously until it spun like a whirlpool. As the swirling liquid slowed to a standstill the sleeping pill powder settled to the bottom once more.

"It's getting kinda wet up here," Eric called from the top of the stairs.

Startled by the sound of his voice, Jessica dropped the spoon in the sink with a clang. "Maybe you should close the doors so the rain doesn't come in," she answered, sweeping the empty capsule shells into her cupped hand and shoving them into the pocket of her jeans. Her stomach fluttered anxiously. "We'll be nice and cozy down here."

Jessica heard the creak of the doors shutting, then a *click* as the latch was put into place. She stood there, hardly breathing, waiting for Eric to walk down the stairs, the tainted iced tea gripped firmly in both hands. A cloud of doom descended on Jessica's shoulders as she stared down at the undissolved powder. It looked so horribly obvious.

"What's he going to do to me when he sees this?" she whispered shakily. The last time she disobeyed, he knocked her out. But in a weird, demented way it was almost as if he'd given her a chance to redeem herself. He could have easily killed her. And Jessica knew, deep down in her bones, that there would be no second chances.

Eric jumped from the top of the steps to the floor, just like a little kid, sending Jessica's already strung-out nerves over the edge. He grinned at her gleefully, apparently thrilled that he'd caught her off guard. "What are you doing?" he asked, pointing to the cup she was clutching in her hands.

"Nothing," Jessica blurted out, raising the tainted cup to her trembling lips. "Just having some iced tea, that's all."

When the circulation returned in his arms and legs, Nick went below deck again. The storm was going full force now, and the sky was completely black except for the jagged bolts of white lightning that streaked through the atmosphere. Despite the flood of water in the cabin, Nick found the light and the shelter from the wind to be a small comfort.

The slight warmth that returned to his limbs gave Nick a renewed sense of purpose. With no rowboat and a radio that he wasn't even sure worked, Nick determined that there was only one solution to his problem.

He'd have to get the schooner sailing again.

Nick knew it was a long shot, but he didn't stop for even a moment to consider his odds. There just wasn't enough time.

"The first thing I need to do is to find out where the water is coming in. Then I have to stop it somehow." Nick remembered Eric saying something about a hole near the galley, so Nick started there. "As if I should believe that creep," he added as he followed along the wall.

But it was as good a place as any to start. Dipping his hands below the waterline, Nick felt for a sudden inflow of water.

Slowly and steadily Nick moved through the water, seeing occasional flashes of lightning through the porthole window and listening to the roar of thunder as it skipped across the waves. Suddenly Nick stopped. "Wait a minute . . . ," he said aloud, feeling a whisper of movement running over the toe of his rubber boot. Kneeling down, Nick stretched his arms out in front of him and felt the cold gush of seawater coming in. Cautiously his fingers searched for the perimeter of the hole, finding at last a nearly smooth opening in the hull, about two feet across.

"Well, I guess Eric wasn't lying about this." Nick traced the leak with astonishment. "This guy is an absolute pro." It wasn't the kind of hole that was caused by an explosion, like Eric had said; it was the kind that was cut, intentionally, with a Skilsaw. As Nick felt along the opening he realized it wasn't one hole, but two. And they weren't even holes at all, but letters. The initials N. F.

Nick Fox. Nick's stomach heaved. *This was a setup. This whole thing . . . he knew exactly who— and where—I was from the beginning. He's trying to kill me.* Nausea suddenly seized Nick as he traced the initials as if they were an epitaph carved into his underwater tombstone. Apparently Eric was hoping to sink the ship as a clean, easy way to dispose of all the evidence—and the detective who was tracking the case. But the psycho couldn't help but add this ironic touch.

"It's not going to happen, Eric," Nick muttered through clenched teeth. "You can't get rid of me so easily."

A new feeling of determination suddenly surged through Nick's veins. Ripping the top of the small dining-room table off its metal center post, he pressed it flat against the holes to keep any more water from coming in. He then pushed a chair against the tabletop to keep it secure.

"There." Nick exhaled loudly. "That should keep the water from coming in for a while."

Taking the hand pump he had brought along, Nick opened one of the porthole windows and threaded the pump's rubber hose through it. He pumped the water manually, the simple contraption making loud sucking noises as he worked. Nick worked as fast as his sore muscles would allow, but the water level hardly budged even a fraction of an inch. There was simply too much water to bail.

After twenty steady minutes Nick slumped against the wall with drops of sweat rolling down his face. "I can't keep this up," he panted, watching tiny pints of water squirting out the window. "At this rate it will take me a week to get the boat running again."

A flash of lightning split the sky and a crack of thunder shook the boat. Wiping the sleeve of his orange jacket across his brow, Nick felt Jessica slipping farther and farther from his reach, like the aluminum boat that had floated out to sea. Time was running out. Soon he would be dead. Most likely Jessica would be too—if she wasn't already.

Eric felt an uncontrollable, almost primitive longing stir within him as he watched Jessica take a seductive sip from the cup of iced tea and hold it out to him like Eve offering Adam the tempting, irresistible apple in the Garden of Eden. "You said you wanted yours sweet," she purred, "but I think I put way too much sugar in. Why don't you try it and tell me what you think?"

Holding back his urges, Eric waved her away, his heart pounding like the pulsating beat of the rain up on deck. "No, thanks. I had some water when I was up on deck. I'm not really thirsty anymore."

"Oh . . . ," Jessica mumbled. Her chin fell against her chest and her lower lip pouted slightly. Tears glistened in her eyes.

Sliding into the dining booth, Eric rolled his eyes. *Why do women act so weird sometimes?* he wondered to himself. "For goodness' sake, Jessica," he said, propping his bare feet up on the table. "Don't cry over it."

"It's just . . . it's just that . . ." Jessica whimpered like a two-year-old. "It's just that I went through a lot of trouble—I was trying to impress you and all, and now you don't even want to try it."

"That's just the way it goes, babe. You're just going to have to get used to it."

Jessica blew her nose into a paper napkin, her face red and shiny with tears. "I know. Nick used to say the exact same thing every time I tried to do something special for him—"

"Nick used to say the same thing?"

"All the time . . ." Jessica drew in a shaky breath. "I'm sorry, Eric. It's just that every time I think I'm getting used to being disappointed, I get upset all over again."

You're such a jerk, Fox. You deserve everything that's coming to you, Eric thought, his stomach clenching like a tight fist. *Jessica's lucky I came along to take her away from you.* He sat up and held his arm out toward her. "Give me the cup—I'll try it."

"It's all right." Jessica sniffled. "You don't have to."

"I want to. Let me try it."

A radiant smile lit Jessica's ethereally beautiful face. "Really?" She handed him the cup and looked away shyly. "I hope you like it."

Eric regarded the cup soberly. *Did she put a pound of sugar in this thing or what?* he wondered, staring at the thick layer of sugar at the bottom. *It's going to be awful. I'll take a sip— just to make her happy.*

After he held the cup up in a mock toast, Eric touched the liquid to his lips and smiled, suppressing the wince forming behind his eyes. The tea tasted horrible. "Mmmm, delicious," he lied. "That's the best iced tea I've ever had, Jessica. Don't let Nick's abuse get to you. I'm nothing like him . . . nothing like him at all."

Jessica didn't answer. She just stared at him, her eyes wide and her brilliant smile frozen on her face. She was leaning forward slightly, breathlessly waiting for him to finish the whole thing. He'd obviously said the magic words. She was putty in his hands.

I guess I should finish it off to make the girl happy, he decided with a silent groan as he threw back his head and drained the cup.

"Eric, you are such a kidder!" Jessica laughed coyly, tickling him under the chin and trying to keep from recoiling in disgust. They'd been cuddling on the cabin couch for at least twenty minutes, and still Eric showed no signs at all of drowsiness. In fact, his dark eyes were as bright and alert as ever.

"I'm not joking," Eric said, running his fingers up and down Jessica's bare neck. "In college I was the best dancer in my class. I used to go to clubs every weekend and win money in dance contests."

Jessica grimaced behind her fake smile. *I don't like you, I don't care about you, and I don't want to hear about your stupid life.* The words repeated over and over in her head like a mantra, punctuated by the pelting rain up on deck. *All I want is to see Nick Fox again.*

Eric's sleazy fingers were working their way down to the neckline of Jessica's T-shirt, stroking the skin underneath. Jessica chewed at the inside of her cheek so she wouldn't cry. *What is* wrong *with you?* she asked silently. *When are you finally going to fall asleep?*

Jessica cleared her throat to cover up the gag forming there. "Did you want to become a professional dancer?" she asked while Eric's lecherous hands wandered all over her.

"No, it was just a hobby," Eric breathed into her hair. "I really wanted to be a karate champion. Full-contact kick boxing was my specialty."

That explains the door, Jessica reasoned.

"How did you do?"

"I was undefeated. Top ranked in the state."

"That's amazing!" Jessica shouted, fully aware that she was probably laying it on too thick but no longer caring—he seemed to like it that way. "Oh, Eric, I'm so proud of you."

Eric's chest puffed up proudly. "It's not that big of a deal. Besides, I had to give it up. It wasn't profitable enough."

"So what did you do instead?"

"I've been doing a little freelance work for the rich," Eric answered mysteriously. Before Jessica had a chance to ask another question, Eric's hands wandered into unwelcome territory.

Luckily for Jessica, a loud clap of thunder sounded and she jumped to her feet, getting as far across the cabin as she could.

"What's the matter?" Eric asked, looking irritated. "We were just getting cozy."

"I'm sorry," Jessica apologized, trying to catch her breath. "I hate thunder. That one really caught me off guard."

Eric patted the empty seat next to him. "Come back here," he said, his voice thick with barely concealed moans. "I'll make you forget all about it."

The thought of getting close to Eric again made Jessica violently nauseous. "I can't sit still.

Thunderstorms make me really nervous," she said. "I have a better idea. Why don't you teach me some of those dance moves you were talking about? I'll run up on deck and grab the radio before the rain totally ruins it. That way we can have some music."

Eric stood up. Tight lines were forming around his eyes and mouth, and Jessica wondered if maybe he was catching on to her. "No, I'll go up on deck since you're such a fraidycat."

"It's OK, really. I'll just be a minute." Jessica dashed for the stairs without looking back to see if Eric was behind her. When she reached the deck, she slammed the doors to the entrance shut and rammed a heavy deck chair under the doorknob.

Heavy winds and sheets of rain assaulted Jessica as she backed away from the entrance. Seconds later Eric's fists pounded against the doors, nearly breaking the flimsy wood from its hinges. "If I were you, Jessica, I'd run and hide," he screamed at the top of his lungs. "Because I'm coming to get you!"

Chapter
Twelve

"This is quite the boat," Elizabeth marveled, taking in the racer's high-tech instrument panel and sleek cockpit, which provided welcome shelter from the rain that had just begun to come down. There was even a cabin below. It was the kind of boat that should have James Bond at the helm. But Matt Birch seemed like a pretty good substitute.

Matt beamed proudly and gave the boat a loving pat. "Me and *Midnight Blue* have been through a lot together. During the summer the boat is my home."

"Where do you go?"

"Up and down the coast, mostly. I compete in a lot of races."

Elizabeth managed a smile despite her worry. "That sounds really wonderful," she said, turning an anxious glance toward the radio. "They're still not responding?"

Matt shook his head. "I don't think their radio is working at all."

It was as if Elizabeth's worst fears had been confirmed. Nick's face flashed in her mind's eye, shaking Elizabeth with rage. *I don't care if you are a cop, Nick,* Elizabeth seethed internally. *If you so much as hurt one hair on my sister's head, I'll see to it that you're brought to justice.*

"There's something else we can do," Matt suggested, making adjustments on the instrument panel. "We can check the radar to see where they're at. They'll probably be pretty easy to find. I don't imagine that too many people would be crazy enough to be sailing in this kind of weather."

"Let's check it out," Elizabeth answered, scooting next to Matt. While she tried to concentrate on the flashy radar display, she couldn't help noticing how his skin smelled of a tantalizing mix of salt air and coconut suntan lotion.

Matt spotted two green blips on the screen in a matter of seconds. "Got 'em."

"This is even better than the equipment the Coast Guard had," Elizabeth said.

"A racer's best friend," Matt said with a gentle laugh. "According to this, there are two boats out on the water within a fifty-mile radius.

One of them is heading slowly in a southeasterly direction and the other one . . ." Matt trailed off and peered at the screen, a strange look on his face.

"What is it?" Elizabeth asked. Her throat felt like it was closing up on her. "What's wrong?"

"Well, this other boat looks like it's stalled or something," Matt answered. He wrote a few notes down on a piece of paper. "There's a chance it could've capsized in the storm that's raging out there."

"Oh no!" Elizabeth clasped her hands to her mouth, and her eyes welled with fresh tears. A capsized boat—that would explain everything.

All along I've been blaming Nick when maybe he didn't do anything at all, she realized. But it was too soon to be sure. Still, the one thing Elizabeth *did* know was that there was much more to the story than she had guessed.

Matt placed an awkward, reassuring hand on Elizabeth's shoulder. "Don't get upset just yet. We don't even know if it's them."

"If they capsized, they're going to need help," Elizabeth cried. "What am I supposed to do?"

"Well, you've got me and *Midnight Blue*," Matt said almost shyly. "We could go out looking for them if you want. With the conditions, though, it could take about an hour or more to get to them."

Elizabeth looked up at the black sky. The rain was sprinkling down in misty drops, and as night began to fall, visibility was almost nil. "You said it was too dangerous to go out there—"

"Too dangerous to go joyriding," Matt corrected. "But it's never too dangerous to help someone in need."

"I can't ask you to—"

Matt held up his hand to silence her. "Please. Don't think twice about it. This boat is so souped up, it can practically run itself. It has a huge outboard engine, so we don't even have to worry about trying to fight the wind." He smiled warmly. "Are you convinced yet?"

Elizabeth wiped her tears away with the back of her hand. "All right," she answered. "Let's go."

"Stay away from me, Eric!" Jessica screamed at the blocked door through the roar of the storm. "I don't want your filthy hands near me!"

Eric grunted as he slammed what sounded like his entire body against the door. "Dirty little tramp!"

The pent-up anger Jessica had been holding inside her for hours was now breaking free. Her voice was hoarse with rage. "I hate you, Eric! I've always hated you! The only reason I pretended to like you was so I could help save Nick!"

"You can forget about your detective boyfriend, Jessica. He's dead," Eric said with an evil laugh that racked her spine with fear. "Just like you'll be in a few minutes!"

Nick! Jessica skidded across the rain-soaked deck to the steering wheel and turned the ignition key to start the boat's motor. Putting the motor in full throttle, she made a sharp bank right, cutting cleanly across the rough surf until the boat was turned completely around. The rain riddled Jessica with the high velocity of machine gun bullets.

A loud *thud* sounded from below, as if Eric had lost his balance in the turn. "What the hell are you doing?" he screamed.

He's going to break out of there, Jessica thought in panic. *I just know it.* As soon as the yacht was on course Jessica grabbed a second deck chair for added security. Just as she was carrying it over to the cabin doors, her toe caught hold of something and she fell to her knees. The deck chair flew from her rain-slick hands. Painfully Jessica got to her feet and looked back at what had tripped her.

It was the dart gun.

Jessica laughed almost giddily to herself. "He left it up here," she whispered under her breath. "I'm home free!"

Sliding the strap over her head, Jessica checked the chamber to see that it was loaded. For the little she knew about dart guns, it seemed fine. In her mind's eye Jessica pictured Nick on the sinking schooner, frightened and sick with worry as the boat sank down into the sea. Then, just as Nick reached the depths of his despair, the *Halcyon* would come barreling through the fog with Jessica at the bow. He'd cry out for joy, proud and amazed at Jessica's quick thinking and impeccable sense of direction. Nick would take her into his arms and promise never to leave her again. And then he'd reward her bravery with a kiss so hot, it would make her knees melt and warm her rain-chilled heart.

Jessica sighed dreamily. *This is going to be the most incredible reunion ever,* she told herself. *Hold on, Nick, I'm coming!*

A loud clap of thunder suddenly snapped Jessica out of her reverie. Eric was still relentlessly hammering at the door. *Sorry, Nick, but before I can save you, I have one certifiable creep I have to take care of,* Jessica added soberly. With the dart gun strapped solidly over her shoulder and gripped firmly in her hands, she walked over to the cabin doors and stood guard, aiming the gun directly in the center.

"Come out here if you dare, Eric," Jessica taunted. "I have a big surprise waiting for you."

So you found the gun, my precious little witch. You must think you're pretty tough. Eric swore savagely at her through the door before heading back down the stairs to get a running start. He bounded up them with the speed of a greyhound, and fueled by a deadly fury, threw his entire weight against the thin doors. The wood gave a little, then bounced back like a spring, throwing him back down the stairs. His limbs pained him only briefly before his adrenaline took over, his eyes turning bloodred with rage.

"You can't do this to me!" he shouted, throwing a bloodied-knuckle punch at the ceiling. "You can't stop me! Nick Fox is a loser, Jessica! A *dead* loser! I'm all you have left. Think of all the things I can do for you!"

"Like what?" Jessica shouted through the door. "Smacking me around whenever you feel like it? Dancing around like a lame moron? Nick is ten times the man you are! And he's a better dancer too!"

Eric's ego burned with humiliation. Jessica was a deceitful, lying fraud, and he

161

had completely fallen for her shrewish scheme. It was bad enough to be suckered by a girl, but even worse to be had by the one girl he truly believed was meant for him.

I wanted to bare my soul to her, and all the while she was just laughing at me. Eric spit at the wall in disgust. *You're not getting away with this, Jessica. No one humiliates me and lives.*

Eric concentrated on the red river flowing down his swollen knuckle and turned his focus inward, like he did before a kick-boxing match, in order to regain complete control. Consciously he controlled his breathing and slowed down his pulse, letting the energy build steadily until the moment of impact, when it would all explode with atomic force.

"If Nick is such a great man," Eric said, his voice slow and steady, "then how come he's on a sinking ship and I'm here with you?"

On the other side of the door Jessica fell silent for a moment. A sublime smile parted Eric's lips.

"Come on, Jess. I'm waiting for an answer. . . ."

"You've made a big mistake, Eric!" Jessica screamed, her verbal assault unleashing with a Medusa-like fury. "Nick is a cop. He's going to arrest you the moment . . ."

That's my good girl, Eric thought as he

backed away from the doors and ignored her shrieking prattle. *Keep talking. You'll never know I'm gone.*

Eric surveyed the cabin, searching for an alternate escape. There were the porthole windows in the galley, but they were too small. He'd seen the rest of the cabin, and there was little to work with.

But what about the bathroom?

Eric threw open the door and stepped inside the tiny, closet-size space. Overhead, the raging rain grew louder and steadier. Eric looked up and a slow, demonic grin crossed his face. There was a skylight.

It was dome shaped and made of molded acrylic, just wide enough for Eric to fit through. "I've broken boards bigger than you," Eric bragged aloud, then easily punched his bloody fist straight through it. The skylight popped right off in one piece. Eric stepped on the toilet, then the sink, and reached for the opening. His strong arms pulled him up to the skylight with hardly any effort. In a matter of seconds he had wriggled his way through to freedom.

The rain cooled Eric's face and torso and cleaned the blood from his hands. Focused energy pulsed in every part of his body; he was ready to take on any or all challengers. Nothing could stop him—not Nick Fox, not Jessica with her dart gun, not even the storm could take him down. He would not be defeated.

Standing at the bow of the yacht, Eric looked across the deck to the stern where Jessica stood, still keeping watch in front of the door. Her back was turned to him; she was apparently unaware he had found an alternate escape route. The gun was slung over her shoulder, poised for action.

This is going to be fun, Eric thought with glee as he slunk silently across the slippery deck toward the steering wheel.

"You might as well give up, Eric, because it's all over," Jessica shouted at the door.

Eric turned off the ignition and pulled out the key. The motor stopped suddenly, and Jessica turned around. Her beautiful blue eyes nearly popped out of their sockets when she saw Eric standing there, holding the key in his hand.

"You're right, Jessica," he said, hurling the silver key high into the air. "It's all over."

"Don't!" Jessica shrieked as she watched the boat key fly over her head. She jumped up to try to catch it, but the key made a wide, perfect arc beyond her reach, over the yacht railing, and into the briny sea. Grief-stricken sobs burst from Jessica's heaving chest as she watched her last chance to save Nick disappear in the churning waves.

Eric flashed a grin. "Not a bad shot, if I do say so myself."

"You're a murderer! A cop killer!" Jessica screeched so loudly, her lungs ached. Then she stopped herself from continuing along that trail of logic when she heard her own bleak accusations ring out over the wildly pitching boat.

Don't say things like that, she told herself. *Nick's not dead. Nick can't be dead. He's still alive, and you can still save him . . . somehow.*

Jessica threw back her shoulders and held her head high, jabbing the barrel of the dart gun in Eric's direction as if it were a bayonet. "If Nick dies, it's going to be all your fault. You'll rot in jail for even *attempting* to kill a police officer."

"Nick's already dead, honey."

Chapter
Thirteen

_"No!"_ Jessica screamed. "You're lying. Nick's not dead. He's _not!_"

"He _is_ dead, sweetheart. And that's exactly what I've been hoping and praying for," Eric continued, strutting toward Jessica with steady, overconfident steps, like a panther who had cornered its prey. "I've been wanting your boyfriend dead for a long, long time. And now"—he cracked his knuckles—"he's out there, drowned, floating lifelessly on the ocean's surface. He's fish food, Jessica."

"You're _lying!_"

"Might as well face it. I'm all you've got now."

"No! Never! _Never!_" Jessica raised the sight of the dart gun to her right eye and poised the barrel steadily, clenching her teeth. "Don't take another step," she warned, her finger on the trigger. "I swear on Nick Fox's life I'll shoot!"

"That's kind of an empty promise at this point, isn't it?" Eric kept on strolling toward her, not hesitating for a moment. His eyelids seemed to droop a little, and for a moment Jessica thought the sleeping pills were finally kicking in. But instead of dropping to the deck in slumber, he shook his head vigorously like a dog just out of water and held his arms outstretched on either side of him, palms up. He wiggled his fingers as if to egg her on. "Go ahead, Jessica. I'd like to see you do it."

"Don't tempt me, Eric. I'm awfully tempted right now."

"You're tempted? By me? Well, now we're getting somewhere. I hope you're not lying this time, darling." Eric was three feet away from her now. "Come on. I want you to do it. If it'll make it easier for you, I'll stop right here so you can have a good shot." He stood in place and began drawing a circle over his chest with his finger, like a human target. "Right here. I bet you can't make it, though."

"Quiet!" Jessica swallowed hard. Her hands were sweaty, and her breath rasped in her throat. Drops of water streamed down her face and dripped off the ends of her soaked hair. But her grasp on the gun was tight. She wasn't going to let it slip. She knew she was in control—at least, she knew she should have been. But Eric's goading had shaken her resolve. "Go sit down over there where I can see you," she demanded, sounding far less forceful than she'd hoped.

"Aww, you poor, scared, pitiful little creature." Eric started walking toward her again, ignoring her warning. "I gave you a chance to get me, and you didn't even take it. I guess it's my turn now." He loomed nearer. His eyes were red rimmed and glassy, filled with deadly intent. "Jessica's too scared to take a sho-ot," he sang teasingly. "Are you scared of me, Jessica? I hope so. That's how I like my women—scared."

The pressure that had been boiling inside Jessica suddenly exploded. Her shaking, twitching finger pulled the trigger almost on its own. Closing her eyes, she braced herself for Eric's inevitable scream of agony as the dart pierced his chest, but no sound came. After several seconds of silence Jessica's curiosity was too great and she peeked. Eric was standing there, a grin on his face and one dark eyebrow cocked. The dart was nowhere near his chest; it was still safely poised in the barrel.

The gun had misfired.

"Oh no." Terror streaked through Jessica's soul as Eric came toward her. All the color drained from her face as Eric's eyes flamed with malice and his lips pulled back to reveal gleaming, wolflike teeth. "Please don't hurt me, please," she begged, defenseless.

She shrieked when Eric grabbed her by the hair and pulled her head back so far that she automatically released the dart gun from her quaking grip. With his free hand Eric yanked the gun away, breaking the strap over her shoulder. She yelled in pain.

Laughing, Eric threw down the weapon and kicked it out of the way with his foot. He leaned in close, so close that his wet face was almost touching hers. "You really disappointed me, Jessica," he said menacingly, his hot breath violating her pale face. "I thought you were the woman I could spend the rest of my life with. But you're just like all the others. I try to show you ladies a good time, and all you do is spit in my face—or try to shoot me." His voice broke into disturbingly unhinged giggles. "I mean, what kind of gratitude is that? I'm not such a bad guy. It's women like *you* who make me bad."

"It's women like me who know better than to get involved with disgusting trash like you," Jessica snapped, her neck cramping painfully. "I'd rather be dead."

Releasing his grip, Eric took a step back.

"Lucky girl," he said, his wet, black hair plastered to the sides of his face. "It looks like you're going to get your wish."

Jessica looked around, but there was nowhere to go. Behind her was the railing, the boat's engine, and then the sea—nothing else. No weapon to cling to, no safe place to escape to. Her body suddenly felt heavy and weightless all at the same time, as if she could already feel her spirit escaping her body. This was it. Her life was over.

"Good-bye, Nick," she whispered, her fingers gripping the metal railing behind her. "I love you . . . forever." She felt her body let go, almost welcoming death. Anything to escape the endless hell that Eric was putting her through. She hoped it would be quick and painless. But at this point she was prepared to endure anything. Whatever it was, she wouldn't fight it. Eric had put her through enough torture already. She had no energy left.

Tears streaming down her face, Jessica steadied her breathing and closed her eyes. Instantly she recalled Nick's gorgeous face and sparkling jade green eyes, the way he smiled at her, the incomparable way he pressed his lips to hers. She felt his arms around her, comforting her, and in her reverie she returned his embrace, just as she had that first amazing night on the *Halcyon*. The memory of Nick filled her with a warm sense of peace. Soon she'd be with him again. . . .

"Kiaiii!"

The sudden cry made Jessica's eyes fly open involuntarily. Eric had moved back from her a couple of feet, but he wasn't holding the dart gun like she had expected. Instead he was in a wide-legged stance, punching air and exhaling, his muscles drawn taut and his veins bulging in his face and arms. He moved his hands in grand circles, taking in and releasing sharp, controlled breaths. He seemed to be preparing himself for some sort of—

Karate match, Jessica realized. *Oh no—he really is a kick-boxing champ. He's going to kill me with his bare hands.*

"Sayonara, Jessica," Eric hollered, his eyes almost rolling back in his head. "It was nice knowing you." He jumped up in the air and spun around, his right leg jolting upward in a roundhouse kick, ready to bring it down with deadly precision. Jessica closed her eyes once more, trying to concentrate on the memory of Nick's loving face instead of feeling the fatal air swirl around her.

Suddenly a huge, swelling wave crashed against the side of the *Halcyon,* making the boat lurch. Opening her eyes in surprise, Jessica caught a glimpse of Eric landing his jump far from its intended mark. His kicking leg wobbled, causing him to rotate clumsily on the slippery, tilting deck. She saw his ankle twist a little, and he fell against the railing, his eyes locking onto hers for an eternally long moment—Eric's dark eyes were filled with shock and humiliation while Jessica's blue ones widened at this new and gloriously unexpected opportunity.

Instinctively her mind dictated her actions the instant before her body carried them out. She skidded over to where the dart gun lay on the deck. Even if it didn't work in the conventional sense, it had an altogether different purpose that Jessica suddenly found very comforting. She picked it up and held it, confident that now, at last, she had the upper hand. She pointed the barrel at Eric just to tease him.

He sneered. "You'd never—"

"*Psych!*" Jessica cried, flipping it around so that the heavy butt of the gun was leveled right at his head. "Good-bye yourself, Eric."

Jessica drew the gun back and knocked him upside the head with every ounce of strength she had, multiplied by her desire for revenge for all the physical agony and mental torture he had put her through. The boat rocked and tilted, gravity working in her favor, and seconds later both of Eric's feet were off the deck, his mouth opening in silent horror. The blackness of his unrelentingly evil eyes bored into her like searing coals as his head smacked against the metal railing, knocking him unconscious. Jessica backed away, covering her face with her hands, as she watched Eric's lifeless body fall into the surging waves.

"This pump isn't getting me anywhere," Nick said aloud, slumping in exhaustion against the galley counter. He had resumed bailing in hopes of getting the schooner sailing again, but his efforts were fruitless. Rain was falling in from the opening at the top of the cabin stairs faster than Nick could pump it out the porthole. It was time to face the grim reality—the boat wasn't going anywhere.

Of course Eric must have been pulling a fast one when he "called" the Coast Guard, Nick realized, his blue lips shivering in the black water that was now up to the middle of his chest. He wanted to kick himself for not paying closer attention when he'd had the chance. But Jessica was right—he was in vacation mode.

Still, Jessica should have had a chance to call them herself by now, he thought. He hadn't heard a boat or a plane nearby, but the thunder and crashing waves would've made it hard to hear anyway. *I hope she was able to—not for my sake, but for hers. She's an amazing, crafty woman. I'm sure she found a way.*

Almost like a sign, the green plastic safety kit Nick had brought along with him floated by. "Flares!" Nick said aloud, grabbing the kit. There were emergency flares in the kit and, if he was lucky, a pack of waterproof matches. If the Coast Guard was anywhere in the vicinity, they'd see the bright flares in the sky and come rescue him.

Nick exhaled hesitantly, not allowing himself to be lured into the feeling of comforting relief that was nipping at his heels. It was too early to settle back and relax. He'd been disappointed too many times before, and Nick didn't think he could take it again.

With the box tucked under his arm, Nick headed for the stairs. The boat was rocking violently now against the churning waters, making Nick wonder how much of the deck was still above-water. Gale winds whistled through the cracks, pounding the craft with a near-hurricane force. Nick forced his freezing, tired legs up the stairs, wondering when the ordeal would be over, and more important, how it would all end.

Almost there, Nick thought, spurring on his weary body as he neared the top. Through the opening he saw the sprawling, powerful hands of the night sky, puffy and black, shot through with electric veins of white lightning. *There's no fighting the tremendous force of nature,* Nick realized. Tossing aside his only weapon, the pump, he surrendered.

Then, as if the storm had noticed him giving in and was ready to gloat about its victory, a monstrous crest appeared near the opening, colliding with the schooner. Nick fell back into the flooded cabin, his emergency kit soaring through the air behind him as the boat tossed and lurched. The entire watercraft tilted back in the opposite direction, and the doors at the cabin stairs swung shut.

Nick resurfaced in a panic. "I have to get out of here," he panted, reaching for the emergency kit. "This boat's going to crack pretty soon. I have to get out!"

Adrenaline burst through Nick's body as he leaped up the stairs. Arms outstretched in front of him, he pushed against the cabin doors. They didn't move.

"Come on!" Nick shouted, ramming his shoulder against the doors. They still wouldn't budge.

He was trapped.

Nick stared at the doors, disbelieving his own rotten luck. Then something inside him snapped. It was that thin, silver wire of hope he had been carrying in his heart through the entire ordeal, the one thing that had kept him going when things were bad. Nick's hope had been stretched and pulled, drawn thinner than he'd ever imagined possible, and now that wire was broken beyond repair. Nick had never been more certain in his entire life that he was going to die.

The schooner creaked and groaned in the tossing waves, shifting from side to side. Cracks started appearing in different parts of the cabin as the water forced its way in. One by one snakes of water appeared, slithering into the murky water.

It's time to stop fighting, Nick thought, giving into the drowsiness that permeated the depths of his entire being. He settled back, letting his muscles relax as the water level in the cabin rose higher and higher.

Jessica watched Eric's sinking body as it submerged beneath the bubbling white sea-foam and slowly disappeared out of sight. She leaned against the railing like a limp rag doll, her tired and wrung-out body overcome with relief while her reeling mind struggled to comprehend what had just taken place.

I killed Eric!
I just killed another human being!
Oh no—how could I—I can't believe—

What's going to happen to me?

It hardly mattered that her own life had been in danger or that Eric had even wanted her dead. Right now, as the adrenaline wore off, Jessica realized that above all else, she was frightened. Not for herself, but for Eric.

"But I didn't kill him," she told herself as she paced the deck, rubbing her hands over her goose-bumped, ice-cold arms frantically. "I just hit him with the gun. I didn't mean for him to go overboard. I didn't mean for him to die. I didn't!"

Her stomach clenched as she imagined the horrific terror Eric must have felt as his last breath left him, then his violent struggle to hold on, trying to remember things about his life, things that were good. Things that he would carry with him into the blackness of eternal sleep.

And as he sank deeper and deeper into the water his lungs would finally contract in a spasm, forcing him to open his airways to the brutal sting of seawater, until finally, irrevocably, he would be—

Dead.

Jessica sat down on the deck and curled her knees up to her chest. She wrapped her arms around her legs and rocked back and forth uncontrollably. "I had to do it," she reasoned, trying to shake off the crushing guilt that was weighing upon her soaking-wet head. "That could've been me."

But it wasn't you, whispered a stronger voice from deep within her. *Eric's gone, and there's nothing you can do about it. You'll have to face the consequences later. Right now you have to worry about saving yourself—and Nick.*

"Nick!" Jessica cried desperately, her voice evaporating into the stormy darkness. All day she had been looking for the moment when she'd be able to bring the yacht back to the schooner and rescue her boyfriend. But now that the moment was upon her, Jessica didn't have the slightest idea where to begin.

The *Halcyon* bounced and rocked like a bucking bronco, completely out of control in the chaotic waves. The deck was as black and slick as oil as Jessica stumbled to her feet and headed across to the other side of the yacht to take control. With feet spread apart and hands braced tightly on the wheel, Jessica fought to keep her balance on the unpredictable deck. Foam-crested waves curled up and tumbled over the railing, splashing Jessica in a violent, un-nerving assault.

I have no idea where I'm going, Jessica realized as she stared out at the unbounded inky blackness. There were no markers to watch, no visible coastline to follow, no other boats to guide her. The sky and sea were one vast, seamless dome, as if she and the boat were inside the belly of a giant black monster that had swallowed them whole. The darkness was endless and terrifying, oppressive and suffocating at the same time. Jessica felt it oozing down around her like thick tar, pressing against her aching ribs and throat. It was going to eat her alive.

Maybe I can figure out this radar thing, Jessica thought. She blindly touched the control panel in front of her, randomly punching buttons and flipping switches. One of the buttons she hit turned on the tiny white-and-blue light on the edge of the yacht while another illuminated a strong floodlight at the bow. Jessica started to breathe a little easier as the pressing darkness subsided. The powerful beam would guide her along in the darkness like a beacon of hope. But after several minutes of working the switches, the radar still refused to come on.

Eric probably wrecked it when he pulled out the radio wires, Jessica reasoned. *It doesn't really matter anyway—I don't have a clue how it works.*

Suddenly the yacht dipped severely to the starboard side, then was tossed easily into the air like a bath toy by an enormous wave. Jessica held on with all her strength, sipping the damp air with short, panicked breaths to ward off the sour green nausea that ate at her torso and clouded her head. Again the boat dipped and bucked into the air against another wave, landing with a pounding splash. The yacht was caught in the trough and would he tossed endlessly unless she figured out a way to turn the boat so it could hit the waves head-on. Jessica's wide, frightened eyes looked up at the mast as it arced against the sky like an erratic pendulum. If she didn't do something soon, the *Halcyon* was going to capsize.

Maybe if I get some speed going, I could control the boat easier, Jessica thought. Automatically her hand reached down to turn the engine key. At the very same moment that Jessica's cold, wet fingers found the empty ignition switch, the not-so-distant memory of Eric's gleeful face as he threw the keys overboard returned, burning itself indelibly in her mind, almost as if he were mocking her from beyond his watery grave.

Chapter Fourteen

"Are you happy, Eric?" Jessica screamed into the swirling wind. She sank to her knees, exploding in a flood of gut-wrenching sobs. "You win, OK? You win after all. Nick and I are going to die—and it's all because we tried to *help* you, you maniac!"

If Nick isn't dead already . . .

The thought popped in Jessica's mind before she could stop it. *Don't think like that,* Jessica scolded herself. *He has to be alive. He is alive. Yes, and I'm going to save him.*

It was the only thing that had kept her going from the moment Nick set off in the flimsy aluminum rowboat. When Eric's threatening screams had shaken the cabin doors, it was the thought of Nick's gentle voice that calmed her fears. When Eric's eager hands had wandered all over Jessica's body, it was the memory of Nick's sweet touch that kept her sane. And when Eric tried to take her life, it was the image of Nick's tender, beautiful face that gave her hope.

But that was a long time ago, and her hope was nearly gone. Hours had passed—how long could he possibly survive on a sinking schooner? Maybe he had jumped on the rowboat instead, but seeing how the yacht was being thrown in the waves, Jessica doubted the rowboat could withstand the storm.

Painful sorrow pierced Jessica's heart like splintered glass. Sobbing uncontrollably, she raised her head to the rainy sky and shouted above the roar of thunder, "Please give me a sign, Nick! Something so that I know you're still alive. Please!"

Jessica waited while the cold, hard raindrops mingled with her tears, but no sign appeared. Not even a single bolt of lightning flashed across the sky. She continued to wait, patiently, not knowing what else to do.

And then it came.

It was so soft at first that Jessica nearly thought she'd imagined it. It was the wind whistling softly in her ears, speaking as gently as Nick's own voice. Jessica stopped crying for a moment, comforted by the sweet hum in her ears. Then, almost magically, the wind seemed to whirl and swirl tightly around Jessica, but she wasn't afraid. The air was tender and warm and safe—the way it felt to be in Nick's arms. It nearly lifted Jessica to her feet and supported her against the turbulent ocean. And then, up in the sky, Jessica thought she saw two gleaming stars as green and beautiful as Nick's eyes. She knew that wherever Nick was, he was trying to show her the way.

Jessica's heart surged with the overwhelming presence of love that surrounded her but fell again as she glanced at the silent motor at the back of the boat. "Please . . . I don't know how to get to you," she whispered. "Show me what to do."

The answer came so easily. She had to sail the yacht herself, just like Nick had taught her.

Jessica stared up at the complicated rigging, the spiderweb of ropes no more understandable to her than it had been the day they had set sail. She wanted to kick herself for not paying more attention to Nick when he was showing her how to handle the yacht. But that was the past; there was no time for regret. Jessica cleared her mind and opened her heart to whatever the wind was trying to tell her.

Seeing the mainsail luffing in the breeze, Jessica instinctively walked to the stern of the yacht and reached for the rudder. Confidently she turned the boat around, steering the bow into the waves. As the yacht reached the sail zone the boom swung across the deck and the mainsail puffed against the wind, pushing the yacht forward toward the green lights.

"Hold on, Nick," Jessica whispered to the wind as confidence and calm flowed through her. "I'll be there soon."

Nick knelt on the galley counter and pressed his head against the cabin ceiling, the water now up to his chin. The pocket of air wouldn't be good for much longer—once it reached his mouth, he'd have to breathe only through his nose, and once it reached his nose, he'd have to tilt his head back—and Nick had no idea how long he could last that way.

Water was pouring in from everywhere now, bursting through the broken porthole windows, trickling through cracks in the wall, raining down from leaks that formed zigzag patterns across the ceiling. Nick was no longer frightened by the sound of the water coming in. To his drifting, cloudy mind it was as beautiful and musical as a tropical waterfall.

Even the cold didn't bother Nick anymore. Below his shoulders there was no longer any feeling, just a vague, pulsating warmth. He couldn't focus on any specific feeling or body part—it was as if all the molecules in his body had drifted away from one another, flowing freely in and around the water, until they were all part of the same organism. Nick didn't know where he stopped and where the water began.

It's getting warm. . . . It's getting so warm. . . .

Nick's eyelids became leaden, and he imagined he was in some exotic, idyllic land untouched by time or the brutal hand of humanity. There was a joltingly loud roar—*A rhinoceros? A lion?* Nick wondered—and then the schooner groaned and shifted, tilting the water level higher in his corner until it touched Nick's bottom lip. A rusted pipe broke, and the cool, tropical waterfall started to run down Nick's head.

It's so nice here. . . . It's so relaxing. . . .

Nick remained completely still in his soothing cocoon of water, watching the tranquil mist that was settling around him. Somewhere in the back of his mind something told him that he had to try to leave, but he didn't exactly remember why. He quickly dismissed the thought. Why on earth would he have to leave such a wonderful place?

Jessica. Nick nearly sighed out loud as he pictured her sarong-clad figure materializing in the mist. But to his dismay, it quickly disappeared.

Jessica would love it here, he thought groggily. *I want her to come here.*

Nick's lips were starting to fall below the waterline, but that was fine with him. He wanted to give himself to the water, to let himself go completely into the beautiful utopian land where he and Jessica could be together, alone, forever. He closed his eyes again and listened to the sweet music of the crystal blue-green water falling through the rain forest. Sublime birds with red, blue, and yellow feathers perched on Nick's shoulders, chirping songs of love. Tender green palms bent for him, weaving their fronds together into a roomy hammock for two. It was paradise.

If only Jessica were here to share it with me . . .

"She *is* here," chirped one of the birds. "She's waiting for you behind the golden doors."

Nick had seen the doors before. They were through the mist and at the top of a hill—huge, solid gold doors that never moved.

"I can't open the doors," Nick moaned lazily. "I can't get to her."

The blue bird flapped his wings. "Then you'll never see her again."

"What do you mean?"

"If you don't try to open the doors right now, you will forever remain on this side and

Jessica will remain on the other," the yellow bird chirped.

Nick blew bubbles in the water. "That's not fair!" he cried. "I tried to open the doors before and I couldn't do it. . . ."

The red bird dug his talons into Nick's shoulder. "You forgot the post . . . under the dining table. . . . It can help you push open the doors."

"And once I open the doors, Jessica can come back here with me?"

"No," corrected the yellow bird. "You have to stay with her on the other side. You can't come back for a long time."

Nick swallowed a mouthful of water, nearly choking. "Wait a minute. . . . I don't know if I want to leave here. . . ."

"Then you'll never see Jessica again," the blue bird said flatly.

But I have to see her again. . . . I can't be without her. . . . Nick started to cry.

The yellow bird ruffled his feathers. "Don't you love her?"

"More than anything," Nick answered sadly. "She's the most important thing in my life. I love just being near her—looking into her beautiful eyes, listening to her laugh, feeling her arms around me. . . ."

"Then get the post!" the three birds chimed in unison.

The post . . . the post . . .

Nick obeyed the order, diving beneath the clear water. His arms pushed ahead of him and his legs kicked mechanically as he swam around dancing bands of sea kelp and transparent jellyfish, schools of darting orange fish and gliding electric eels. He dove deeper still, brushing against the fine sandy bottom with stingrays and octopus until he came upon a mound of pink brain coral with a gleaming silver post in the middle.

Nick twisted and pulled the post until it came loose from its anchor at the bottom of the sea, and he swam with it toward the hill leading to the doors. *I have to see Jessica again,* Nick thought, struggling against the beauty and tranquility of the water and the fish and the birds. No matter how wonderful paradise was, it was nothing without Jessica.

Nick's numbed feet found the stairs and he bounced up, buoyed by the saltwater. The swirling tropical colors faded and turned gray and the gilded doors melted into wood. Still submerged, Nick held out the post in front of him like a huge silver sword, and with a tremendous burst of energy he plowed ahead. The post made solid contact against the doors and they gave way under the pressure, revealing more blackness behind them.

He fought against the pouring current, bracing himself against the doorframe and pushing himself up to the surface of the black water, his lungs burning for oxygen. He tilted his head toward the rainy, open sky and gasped. He found air. He was home.

Eric sank into the dark void as if he were slipping into a black hole. Gravity seemed to be collapsing beneath him, so that he hardly knew which way was up. He felt horribly tired, as if he could sleep forever. Maybe he *was* sleeping. There was no sound, no light, no real sense or feeling, only a tremendous nebulous force that was attacking him in all directions—tearing him apart limb by limb.

Jessica! Help me! Eric tried to scream, but his words disappeared into the vacuum with no form of transmission. Blackness filled his mouth and nose, making its way into his lungs. A sudden violent shift and his body was turned around again, spinning him deeper into the abyss.

What's happening to me?

Eric felt something tugging at his elbow. It lifted him slightly from the black emptiness, then dropped him again even deeper. Rising and falling, rising and falling all over again, pulling and tugging, like a gigantic sea dragon that caught him on one of its enormous scales. Eric didn't have the strength to fight against it. Legs and arms outstretched, head rolling backward, he let the forces take him wherever they desired. Then suddenly there was a strong tug.

I feel something. . . .

Eric's spinning head was jolted from its stupor. The pain came from his elbow and radiated up his arm to his shoulder with such savage intensity, Eric thought his arm was going to be ripped from its socket. His tortured howls evaporated soundlessly into the empty atmosphere. He had never felt so lost and alone in his entire life.

If only Jessica were here with me. . . .

The back of Eric's head throbbed in hot pain as he tried to picture Jessica's beautiful hair and eyes, the way the sunlight played upon her skin. He saw her standing there on the deck, staring at him with wide eyes . . . then he saw her coming at him, almost running with her arms outstretched. . . . *She wants to hold me.* . . . But no—that wasn't it at all. There was something in her hands, something she swung with a force he never in a million years would have believed she had.

She hit me. She pushed me overboard.

Eric relived first the hard smack of the dart gun, then the equally painful crack of the railing against the back of his head. The last thing he remembered was seeing Jessica looking down at him as he faded into the blackness. The devil inside her had pushed its way out of her angelic face and body. She was evil.

She pushed me. . . .

The realization of what Jessica had done cut him so deeply that Eric hardly noticed the tortuous pain that was racking his body. There was no physical pain that Eric couldn't handle—but betrayal, especially from the woman he loved, the woman who should have been his soul mate, was worse than death.

Still being dragged by his arm through the impenetrable darkness, Eric felt himself suddenly being lifted higher and higher until a strange blast of air ripped into his lungs and loud rushing sounds rang in his ears. Then as he fell again, the silence returned. He sank deeper and deeper, and just when he thought he was about to reach the bottom of the black hole, he was yanked back up into the earsplittingly loud air all over again.

Let go of me!

Eric's arms flailed wildly as he tried to release himself from whatever it was that was viciously dragging him. His hand smacked against smooth metal, then flat wood. The strange object lurched forward suddenly, and Eric used the momentum to pull himself a little closer, holding on to it. Blindly he felt two metal tubes about two feet across joined by a series of flat wood slats . . . a ladder. Yes, it was definitely a ladder.

He blinked away the saltwater of the ocean, which had overwhelmed his tears, and looked up.

The ladder was attached to the yacht.

The *Halcyon*.

Throwing his head back in victory, Eric purged the water he had swallowed and gulped at the fresh air. *I'm alive!* he wanted to scream. *I'm alive! No one can kill me—not even you, Jessica Wakefield!*

Eric's eyes adjusted to the black of night, catching shadows of the white cresting waves around him, of the silent motor next to him, and of the simple yacht ladder that had saved him from drowning. Eric drank in the soothing night air, praising the silver stars that were shining down on him.

Did you hear that, Jessica? Eric thought happily as he held onto the boat in tow. *I'm back, and I can't wait to see you again.*

Wrapped in a wool blanket, Elizabeth sat at the bow of the racer, watching the first light of dawn breaking on the horizon. It was a thin, orange-red band of light wedging itself between the black ocean and sky. The rains had stopped hours ago. Now the winds were beginning to subside and the seas were calm once more. But anxiety and fear still raged inside Elizabeth, setting every nerve in her body permanently on edge, every reflex and instinct in survival mode. She had spent the entire night replaying the events of the previous day, trying to remember every word Jessica said and every sound that was made, as if it would somehow give Elizabeth a clue to her sister's fate. But she was still no closer to finding the answer.

Elizabeth pushed aside a strand of hair that had blown across her furrowed brow. She was positive now that something horrible had happened to her sister. Her only hope was that she wasn't too late.

Unfortunately the trip had taken a lot longer than Matt had anticipated. The waves were so strong and the fog so dense that they could only go a few miles an hour. But now Matt had *Midnight Blue* in full throttle and the blue racer sailed effortlessly over the waves, spending more time in the air than on the surf.

"We're getting really close!" Matt shouted to her above the roar of the engine.

Elizabeth jumped down from her perch into

the cockpit and looked at the radar panel. "Which one is it?"

"The stalled one," Matt answered, his sandy hair whipping back in the wind. "But the other one has changed its course and is moving closer to us." Matt squinted in concentration as the orange sunlight cast a perfect glow on his handsome features. The slightest tired shadow fell under his crystal eyes and tiny lines edged his soft mouth. The stormy night had definitely taken its toll on his good looks.

Elizabeth placed a gentle hand on his forearm. "In case I didn't say it already, thank you for doing this."

"Anytime, Elizabeth," Matt answered with a humble smile. "Anytime."

Folding her arms anxiously across the front of her Windbreaker, Elizabeth turned her attention away from Matt and stared out at the sea. As the blip on the radar moved closer to the center of the screen Elizabeth spotted a large dark object dappled with the sun's gold rays, floating in the calm water. It seemed lumpy and round, more like a rock or a whale than a boat.

I can't believe it, Elizabeth thought, a sinking feeling settling in her stomach and sending a chill of fear through her bones. *We've been chasing the wrong thing all along.*

Chapter Fifteen

"That's not what we're after, is it?" Elizabeth cried, pointing at the bizarrely shaped mass floating out in the water.

"I'm afraid it is," Matt answered. "It's hard to see in the early morning sun. Why don't you take a look through these?" He handed her a pair of binoculars.

Focusing the lenses, Elizabeth instantly saw that it was indeed a boat. "Oh no!" she shrieked.

"What's wrong?"

"It capsized!" Elizabeth tried to hold the binoculars steady in her shaking hands, but she dropped them to the deck with a loud bang. Mumbling a quick apology, she snatched the binoculars back up again and looked through them, thankful that the lenses hadn't broken.

197

"Is it your sister's boat?" he asked.

Elizabeth swallowed hard, staring at the looming shape with trepidation. "I can't tell. All I can see is the bottom of the boat. Only half of the hull is above-water—" Elizabeth's breath came in short rasps as her pulse quickened. "Matt—I think it's sinking!"

Matt's jaw fluttered a bit, but the rest of his face remained stoic and calm. "It could be an abandoned boat, but we'd better take a look just to be sure."

Dropping the binoculars by her side, Elizabeth was gripped by an icy feeling of terror that dripped into her veins slowly but certainly. Now that she was closer than ever to finding out the truth, Elizabeth suddenly realized she was too frightened to face it. She knew in her heart that what happened to Jessica was so terrifying and horrible that the simple thought of it would be enough to drive her insane. It would almost be better never to know.

In a fit of panic Elizabeth pulled desperately at Matt's arm. "Turn the boat around!"

"What's wrong?" Matt's eyes narrowed with concern.

Pressing her face against his arm, Elizabeth started to cry. "I can't handle this—I don't want to see—"

"Shhh," Matt soothed, stroking the top of

her head. "Everything's going to be all right. We don't even know for sure if this is Jessica's boat."

"I can't do it, Matt. Please, let's turn around."

"We can't, Elizabeth. What if someone's on board that sinking boat? We have to help them."

Elizabeth knew he was right. Taking a deep breath, she let go of Matt's arm and tried to pull herself together. *What am I doing, clinging to a total stranger like this?* Elizabeth thought, her face burning with embarrassment. She straightened up and brushed aside her tears. "I'm sorry I'm acting like this," she said thickly.

Matt smiled, but it did nothing to hide the anxiety that was lurking in his eyes. "There's no need to apologize."

Elizabeth braced herself against the railing and prepared for the worst. As they neared the wreck she could see large cracks and gaping holes in the hull of the boat where water seemed to be pouring in. At least three-quarters of the boat was underwater, and the rest was sinking fast.

This has to be Jessica's boat. I just know it, Elizabeth thought, her knees weakening beneath her. *This explains everything—the panic in Jessica's voice, the strange splash I heard over the phone, the radio suddenly not working.* She silently scolded herself for thinking the worst of Nick. Of course he would never purposely try to hurt Jessica.

But Jessica did say someone was after her—some man, she reminded herself. *Could Nick's temper have flared up strongly enough to sink the entire yacht?*

Elizabeth shuddered. Staring grimly at the ghostly remains of the boat, she realized the situation was even bleaker and more complex than she ever could've imagined. It seemed as if there was no hope for Jessica—no hope at all.

"I'm going to swing around to the other side," Matt said, steering the racer in a wide circle around the wreck. "You don't have to watch if you don't want to. I'll let you know if I see anything."

Elizabeth swallowed hard, her red, tired eyes brimming with tears. "It's OK," she said stoically. "I'll be all right." But she turned her head anyway, focusing on the clear, brilliant band of yellow sunlight streaming across the horizon.

Matt let the engine idle as they neared the sinking boat. Suddenly he drew in a quick breath of surprise, causing Elizabeth to look over in his direction. "I can't believe this, Elizabeth," Matt cried. "There's a man on the boat."

Elizabeth couldn't believe her eyes either. Squinting in the sunlight, she saw a lifeless body in a bright orange rain suit lying facedown across the fallen masts—only one lifeless body. And it was definitely a man's. There was no one else clinging to the boat, no sign of Jessica anywhere.

She's trapped inside, Elizabeth thought urgently, morbidly. *She's trapped underwater where no one will ever find her.*

"Could that be your sister's boyfriend?" Matt cut the engine and drifted toward the schooner.

Tears rolled down Elizabeth's face as she shrugged limply. "I don't know—maybe." She groaned, her mind no longer able to process her thoughts clearly. All she could dwell on was that orange rain suit. It looked so odd to her, floating in the water as if there wasn't even a real body inside. That couldn't possibly be Nick, could it? No, absolutely not. Even though he was an undercover cop, it was impossible for Elizabeth to picture him in a getup like that.

Overwhelmed by grief, Elizabeth found her last thought bizarrely funny, and she had to stifle a small giggle. But when she saw the figure's legs flopping in the water like a marionette's in the racer's wake, she quickly sobered up. Sympathy tugged at her heart. Whoever the guy was, he had been through a terrible ordeal. "Do you think he's still alive?" she asked, gathering herself together.

"Maybe we'd better find out." Matt waited until the waves drifted *Midnight Blue* toward the schooner, then when they were close enough, he reached out over the side railing and grabbed onto one of the broken masts. He motioned for Elizabeth to come over. "Hold on to this," he said, placing her hands on the mast. "Keep the boat steady. I'm going to try to get him."

"Be careful!" Elizabeth cried. Her stomach tied itself in nervous knots as Matt attempted to rescue the man, keeping one foot on the racer while gingerly placing one foot on a broken plank that stuck out horizontally from the splintered deck. Feeling the strong tug of the current trying to push the boats apart, Elizabeth tightened her grip on the mast and held on with all her strength.

"I think he's breathing!" Matt shouted as he poked and prodded the man. He stepped off the racer so that all his weight was balancing on the pieces of jagged, broken wood that jutted in all directions. The wreck bobbed precariously in the water.

"Be careful, Matt!" Elizabeth's fluttering heart caught in her throat and her muscles strained against the racer's erratic movements. "I don't think it can hold you for much longer. Hurry!"

"Bring the boat closer!"

Elizabeth pulled the schooner's mast, but the racer skidded away diagonally instead of closing the gap. In a brief, terrifying instant she pictured herself losing her grip and then helplessly watching in horror as she drifted out to sea with Matt trapped on the wreck. "I can't do it!" she cried.

"Yes, you can! Move it like this—" Matt motioned in the air to guide her.

Elizabeth followed his instructions, and like a miracle, the gap narrowed between them until there was only two or three feet that separated the racer and the wreck.

"Hold it steady—" Matt stooped and slid the man onto his back, the victim's orange arms dangling off Matt's shoulders. Suddenly there was a loud *crack* as the planks beneath Matt's feet started to give way.

There was no time to warn him, but Matt's eyes widened with fright as if he was completely aware of what was about to happen. In stunned silence Elizabeth watched as the wood cracked and splintered beneath his feet, chips flying in the air, then falling into the water.

What do I do? Elizabeth wondered, racking

her brains for a solution, but her mind seemed frozen and sluggish. Suddenly, thankfully, her reflexes seemed to take over. It was as if Elizabeth's soul had separated from her body and she was witnessing the scene from a safe, detached place up above. She watched her body swerve around the mast and pull the pole toward her, slipping the deck of the racer within inches of the shattered plank so that Matt's next step landed on safe ground.

The momentum from the two bodies was strong, and the two men tumbled onto the deck of the racer with enough force to push the racer away from the sinking wreck. Elizabeth let go of the mast and rushed to Matt's side. "Are you all right?" she asked breathlessly.

"I think so," Matt answered, wearily rubbing the back of his head. "But I think I might've done some damage to this guy."

Elizabeth looked at the man in orange, sprawled out across the floor of the cockpit, his face turned away from her. The fingers of his right hand were twitching slightly, and Elizabeth could have sworn she saw his foot moving. "I think he's going to be OK, Matt," she answered, brushing aside the soft strands of hair that stuck to his sweaty forehead. "You were great."

"So were you." He smiled up at her with admiration.

Elizabeth crouched down and tended to the unconscious man, turning his stirring body toward her so she could take a closer look. But when she saw his face, her heart nearly burst out of her chest and her head instantly went featherlight and dizzy.

"Nick!" she cried, falling back on her heels. "Ohmigosh, no!"

Matt helped Elizabeth regain her balance. "Your sister's boyfriend?"

Elizabeth nodded, not even looking at Matt. She couldn't take her eyes off Nick's face. It was dark and leathery, and his lips were pale blue with dry white wrinkles around the edges. He looked as battered and bruised as the wreck. A loud groaning sound came from out of nowhere. "Nick?" Elizabeth asked, kneeling down and grabbing him by the shoulders. "Nick, where's—"

"No, Elizabeth," Matt said quietly, tapping her on her shoulder and pointing back toward the wreck. Another groan came from the sinking boat as it rolled over in the water until it was nearly upside down.

"*Jessica!*" Elizabeth screamed. Panic flooded Elizabeth's senses like shocking volts of electricity. "Where's Jessica?" she cried, on the verge of hysteria. Her chest was rising and falling as rapidly as the tremulous beats of her heart. "Where is she?"

Matt's face paled. "You don't think she's . . ."

Still on the boat? Elizabeth's stomach churned in anguish as she remembered the horrible scenario she'd dreamed up earlier. Had it actually come true?

"Nick," she whispered urgently, gently slapping both sides of his face to wake him. "Nick, wake up. You need to tell me where Jessica is . . . what you've done with her . . . *now!*"

Nick began to stir slowly. His head rolled from side to side, and his shoulders started to move.

"Nick, please try to wake up." Elizabeth fought to keep her voice steady. "You need to tell me what happened to Jessica. If you've done anything to hurt her, I swear I'll kill you. I swear I will!"

Both arms draped over the yacht ladder, Eric continued to hang on, waiting until he gained enough strength to put his plan into motion. The rains had thankfully stopped, leaving the blustery winds to dry the upper half of Eric's body while his legs were still submerged in the frigid water. A thin film of chalky white sea salt dried in the cracks of his sunburned skin. His mouth and throat were pasty and dry, and his tongue felt as if it were three feet thick.

Eric tried to swallow, but his throat was too

parched. *Water,* he thought. *I need some water.* Reaching up with one hand, he touched the back of his head where he had hit the railing and his brow where Jessica had hit him with the butt of the dart gun. The wounds were already dried and crusted with blood—evidently the saltwater had helped to seal them. Eric smiled to himself. Once again fate was on his side.

Let's see how sweet Jessica is doing on her own, Eric thought, pulling himself up a rung on the ladder until he could see just over the edge on the stern. He squinted a few times to focus. Jessica was near the front of the boat with her back to him, pulling at the jib sheet. The sun's first rays illuminated her hair like spun gold. Despite all she had done to him, Eric was nearly driven mad with desire. He wanted her so desperately, his whole body ached. Jessica was an absolute goddess.

A dead goddess.

Eric's eyes narrowed with fury as the stabbing memory of her betrayal returned. He watched from the ladder as Jessica sailed, completely unaware of what was in store for her. Eric's stomach tingled with excitement, savoring the delicious power he possessed. He could hardly wait.

Jessica dropped the jib sheet and moved farther toward the bow of the *Halcyon.* Eric's dry, cracked hands gripped the top ladder rung with explosive anticipation.

Do it, coaxed a voice inside his head. *You might not get another chance as good as this one. You have to do it now!*

Jessica leaned over the front of the railing and looked down into the water. He could see her lovely brow crease with concern.

Looking for me? he asked silently. *I'm right here.* Eric wanted to laugh out loud, but he couldn't give himself away—not yet. His timing had to be perfect.

As soon as he was certain she wouldn't turn around for a minute or two, Eric put his feet on the ladder and pulled himself up and over the railing. He sprang onto the deck and landed softly on the pads of his feet, as giddy as a child in an amusement park. But the thrill wore off quickly as the hammering pain returned to his head. Eric's muscles were slow to respond as he started his trek across the boat.

Maybe it's too soon, Eric thought, his chest heaving tiredly. But he couldn't stop. It was as if Jessica were drawing him to her like a magnet.

Jessica looked up from the water and turned a little to one side, as if she were about to walk away at any moment. Eric put one foot forward, but his legs were too numb with cold to support him, and he stumbled. *There's not enough time,* he warned himself. *You'll never surprise her at this rate.* He worriedly eyed the dart gun, which was lying in wait in the middle of the boat near the steering wheel. If Jessica spotted him first, she'd definitely win the race to get the weapon. *Wait, Griffin. Just wait for the perfect moment.*

Jessica turned her head and looked out over the port side, making Eric's heart skip a beat. *Did she see me?* he wondered, freezing in place and waiting, watching as Jessica turned her head again toward the bow. He was safe—for now.

Eric lurked stealthily across the deck, searching for a place to hide. Dragging his feet over the water-soaked wood, Eric's toe caught on something that felt like a huge plastic bowl. As Eric reached down to see what it was, a bright smile spread over his face as if he'd just been reunited with an old friend.

It was the bathroom skylight.

Eric located the hole in the deck in a matter of seconds. Quickly, quietly, he sat down on the deck, letting his legs dangle in the hole. *See you later, sweetheart,* he thought, giving Jessica one last look before raising his arms over his head and dropping down into the bathroom. The jagged edges of the hole scraped his body painfully as he went through, leaving long, bloody scratches along his arms, legs, and face. A warm, sticky liquid oozed from the back of his head. The wound from the railing had opened again.

Eric replaced the skylight dome and locked the door. He stared at his bloodied, battered, and exhausted body in the mirror. The stinging crimson rivers streaming down the length of Eric's body made him feel vibrant, alive. The pain only made him stronger.

Soon he would get his revenge, but first he needed to rest and restore his energy. Eric curled up like a cat on the tiny bathroom floor and smiled dreamily as he began to drift off to sleep. Sleep came easily, even more quickly than he thought it would, and before long he was lost in a safe, inky darkness, where Jessica's beautiful eyes bulged with terror and her strangled cries rose from her slender throat and rang gloriously through the air like a symphony.

I hope you're ready, Jessica Wakefield, he thought, his lips curling into a sleepy smile. *You're in for the surprise of your life.*

"Come on, Nick," Elizabeth urged. "Wake up!"

Nick's eyelids flickered a little. He opened them a fraction, just enough so Elizabeth could see his pupils rolling wildly. His dry lips parted as if he were about to speak, but nothing came out but a foggy croak.

"He needs water!" Elizabeth shouted at Matt, her voice harsh with worry.

"I think there's some in the cabin." Matt dashed down the stairs.

Nick lifted a fatigued hand and stroked Elizabeth's cheek, giving her a weary smile. His eyes brightened. "Jessica . . . I was so worried about you."

Elizabeth gently moved his hand away from her. "It's not Jessica, Nick. It's Elizabeth," she answered almost apologetically. Immediately the

211

light seemed to go out in his eyes, and Elizabeth's heart ached for him. She knew instinctively that he hadn't done anything to hurt her sister. "We can't find Jessica. Do you know where she is?"

Matt returned with a plastic jug of water and a cup. Elizabeth propped up Nick's head and shoulders against her knee and gave him some water to drink. When he finished draining two cups, he looked up at her, deep worry lines creasing his forehead. "She's on the boat," he said.

Elizabeth and Matt exchanged frantic glances. All the entrances to the sinking schooner were below the waterline—it was doubtful that anyone in the boat could have survived. Elizabeth had been fighting so long to save her sister's life that on hearing the final news she surrendered calmly, no longer having the strength to deny the truth. With her chin falling against her chest she wept quietly, unable to express the unbearable anguish that was tearing at her heart.

"If only I had been able to get here sooner, I might've been able to save her," she whispered, tears streaming down her cheeks.

"It's my fault," Matt said, placing a sympathetic hand on her shoulder. "I could've done something to get the boat here faster. . . ."

Nick rolled his head toward Elizabeth. "No . . . she's not on this boat," he said in a dry, raspy voice. "She's on the yacht we rented."

"*What?*" Elizabeth cried.

"Jessica's not here. . . ."

She handed Nick another cup of water, then turned to Matt. "Do you think he's hallucinating?" she whispered out of the corner of her mouth.

"He *is* pretty dehydrated, but I don't know," Matt answered. "He seems OK."

Nick tried to stand but fell to his knees. Elizabeth wrapped his arm around her shoulders and eased him up onto a seat. "Nick, try and explain things clearly, OK? I'm not following you. Why is Jessica on another boat?"

"This boat was sinking. . . . I was trying to rescue someone. . . ." Nick paused to take another drink.

The gears in Elizabeth's mind were turning, trying to fit together the little bits of information Nick was tossing out. She wanted to believe what he was saying but was afraid it was all a fantasy Nick had constructed in his delirious state. Elizabeth couldn't risk building her hopes up only to have them be brutally dashed again, so she held on to the grief like a black cloud suspended in her chest, waiting to find out the real answer.

"There is another boat in the area, remember?" Matt said, pointing to the radar. "Maybe that's the boat he's talking about."

Covering Nick with her blanket, she pressed him for answers. "So you're saying Jessica's safe?"

Reviving a little, Nick shook his head. "Eric is with her," he murmured.

"Who's Eric?" Elizabeth asked. When Nick wouldn't answer, her patience broke, and her entire body quaked with confusion. "Tell me, Nick! Who on earth is Eric?"

"It's a long story," Nick began, "but I'll try to make it as short as possible . . . for Jessica's sake."

"Help!" Jessica shouted frantically, waving her arms in the air. "Over here! I need help!"

Jessica had watched the little blue boat skip over the rippling water from the moment it appeared as a tiny dot on the horizon through Nick's powerful binoculars. It was the first other boat she'd seen since before the storm began and, with no sign of Nick or the schooner in sight, she was afraid it was her last chance to save her boyfriend. But even in the binoculars' sights, it looked tiny; when she put down the binoculars, she couldn't see it at all.

"Help! Somebody help me!" Jessica jumped up and down, screaming, hoping with every ounce of her soul that somehow her voice would be carried over to the boat and alert its driver to come to her rescue. But just after the little blue boat had first appeared in her sights, it became rooted to the spot, and Jessica was beginning to think that its inhabitants had no intention of getting any closer to her—in fact, they probably didn't even know she was there.

Nick, I'm trying so hard to get to you. I really am. I've done everything I could—I even killed somebody. And it's not enough! When is it going to be enough? When am I ever going to see you again?

Jessica's lips quivered as she fought to hold back the tears that stung her eyes. She'd tried not to think about what must've become of Nick, all alone out there in the storm. She'd tried not to think about how frightened and cold he probably had been or how long he might've suffered. But what she absolutely could not get out of her head was what Nick's last thoughts might have been. Did Nick realize that Eric was the one who turned the boat around? Or did he think Jessica did it because she was mad he left her behind?

Groaning, Jessica felt as if her stomach were caving in, just from imagining the terrible pain the misunderstanding might have caused him. Had Nick realized that she loved him more than anything in the world? Did he know that she was doing everything in her power to save him?

"I'm so sorry for everything I did, Nick. I'm sorry for all the times I was stubborn and difficult," Jessica cried to the open air. She picked up the binoculars again and watched the blue boat intently, trying to will it to move. But it hadn't budged an inch.

Just when she thought she couldn't cry anymore, big, fresh tears sprang to her eyes and rolled down her face. Guilt pressed down on her painfully like a steamroller, crushing every last bit of hope she had left.

"I failed you, Nick," she cried out loud. "I'm so sorry. . . . I'm so, so sorry. I wish there was some way I could make it up to you—some way to let you know how much I love you . . . but . . . but . . . ."

Bleary-eyed, Jessica watched her tears fall into the cold, deep sea. At the very notion of Nick's death her body became an empty, soulless shell racked with agonizing sobs. "I wish—so much—I could take it all back and start over," she wailed. "If I had you back, Nick, I'd never take you for granted again."

*   *   *

"You left my sister alone with a *murderer?*" Elizabeth shouted in outrage. Nick's unbelievable story had carried her through a draining whirlwind of emotions that left her in a daze. "What were you *thinking?*"

"I didn't know at the time—" Nick's complexion paled to an ash gray. "I made a mistake, OK? I just hope Jessica will . . . will still be able to forgive me."

White-hot anger flared inside Elizabeth's chest. Just when she thought she could taste relief at the realization that Jessica hadn't been trapped on the capsized boat, a whole new set of dangerous variables had been introduced into the equation.

"I hope she'll be able to forgive you, Nick . . . if she's still alive, that is!" Elizabeth shouted cruelly. As soon as the words escaped her she wished desperately that she could call them back. She only wanted to make Nick feel the same searing pain that was burning her insides. But seeing that he now realized he had unknowingly left Jessica stranded on the yacht with a murderous psycho, there was no doubt in Elizabeth's mind that he already did . . . and bringing up the question of Jessica's well-being only made matters more difficult.

Matt started the engine and pulled away from the wreck. "There's no point in arguing about it," he said calmly. "We have to go out there and find her." Swerving the racer 180 degrees, he headed off toward the coordinates indicated by the radar.

Nick nodded solemnly, placing a shaky hand on top of Elizabeth's. "If I had known about Eric, I would've never left Jess alone with him," he said pleadingly. "We wouldn't have even let him on the *Halcyon* in the first place. Please, Elizabeth . . . you have to forgive me. I'm begging you. It's the only hope I have left."

A dark, thick gloom settled over Elizabeth like a shroud. Snatching her hand away, she stood up and walked to the back of the boat. "Bring my sister back in one piece, Nick," she snapped, "and I'll think about it."

"Is it . . . yes . . . *yes!* Oh, thank goodness! Over here! Over here!" Jessica jumped up and down ecstatically. As if by a miracle, the little blue boat had suddenly begun speeding in her direction. In a matter of moments she'd be saved!

But what about Nick? a voice in her head nagged morbidly. *It's too late for him. . . .*

Jessica gulped at the realization. Her spirits crushed in defeat, she settled back into a deck chair and tried to keep the tears from falling once more. Even if the boat was coming to her rescue, it was far too late to do anything for her boyfriend except tell the Coast Guard the general area where they'd most likely find his body.

All the energy and excitement she'd felt for those few fleeting moments had vanished completely in a flash. She no longer wanted to wave or do anything to try to secure the driver's attention. "Whatever happens, happens," Jessica mumbled, not even bothering to look up. "I don't even care anymore. Nothing I do is going to bring Nick back."

A bleating horn sounded twice, making Jessica look up. The blue boat was coming right for her. *It's going to hit me,* she thought with mild alarm, too numbed by grief to react. The boat honked again. Jessica shot an angry glance at the driver. *He can't possibly expect me to move out of the way. I can hardly keep this thing afloat, let alone steer—*

Jessica's thoughts were interrupted by the sight of a familiar blond braid bouncing in the boat. Jessica rubbed her blurry eyes and looked again. *I must be seeing things,* she told herself. *What would Liz be doing all the way out here with a guy in a slick blue racer? I must be hallucinating.*

But then the blond passenger waved. *Is she waving at me?* Jessica looked around again for other boats in the area, but there were none. She raised a hesitant hand and waved. The blond woman waved back excitedly just before the boat came up on her and started to turn.

Jessica ran for the binoculars and looked through them, her jaw falling open in amazement. *I can't believe it!* she thought, staring at the boat in stunned silence. *It is Liz!* The blue boat sidled along the yacht and Elizabeth held out her arm to bring the boats together. A huge, brilliant smile lit up her face.

Jessica reached out and grabbed her sister's arm, feeling Elizabeth's warm pulse beating in time with her own. They stared at each other, blue-green eyes meeting blue-green eyes, glowing smile meeting glowing smile, minds meeting in the mystical bond shared only by twins.

Wherever I go, she finds me. Whenever I'm in trouble, she's there to help me.

Jessica heart overflowed with love for her sister. It was as if she was being rejoined with her other half. But there was still a large piece of her that was missing.

"How on earth did you find me?" Jessica whispered in tearful relief as she helped Elizabeth on board the yacht.

Elizabeth jumped onto the deck and threw

her arms lovingly around her sister's neck. When she pulled away, she motioned to the handsome man who sat behind the wheel of the boat. "Matt here is on the cutting edge of sailing technology. Matt, this is my sister, Jessica."

Matt nodded and gave her a boyish grin. "I gathered as much," he said, waving. "It's nice to finally meet you, Jessica. I'm glad to see you're all right. Your sister was incredibly worried."

Jessica looked at her sister in confusion. "But how did you know that I needed help?"

"The phone call," Elizabeth answered. "You were frantic—I could hardly understand you. But I could tell by the fragments I understood and from the sound of your voice that something out of the ordinary had happened."

Jessica had totally forgotten about the phone call. It seemed as if it had taken place ages ago. The warmth she'd been feeling suddenly drained out of her like a leaky balloon and was replaced by the icy chill of despair. "You absolutely wouldn't believe what's happened to us, Liz. Except that it's not quite over—not yet." Her throat tightened as she spoke. "Nick is—"

"Right here."

A chill rippled through Jessica's body as she slowly turned her head to the racer. Nick's disheveled head and exhausted face peeked out from behind the racer's cabin doors. It was the most beautiful sight Jessica had ever seen in her entire life.

This can't be real, Jessica thought, afraid to believe, afraid once again that she was hallucinating. Elizabeth squeezed her sister's hand and whispered in her ear, "We found him on the schooner before we got to you. He's a little shaken up, but he'll be fine." She stepped aside as if she meant to give them a little privacy. "Especially now that we've found you, he should make a complete recovery."

As if in a dream, Nick walked slowly toward the edge of the racer, his lips trembling. Their eyes locked. Jessica lost herself in the emerald green depths of Nick's eyes, drinking in the glow of love she'd thought she'd never see again. It filled her, washing away all the fear and hopelessness, the guilt that had consumed her for what felt like an eternity. Wordlessly Nick's eyes seemed to be telling her he'd never stopped believing in her love for him. In fact, it was her love that had kept him alive.

Silently Nick stepped onto the deck of the yacht and took Jessica into his arms. Jessica flinched slightly as his strong arms enveloped her, almost frightened by the explosive, bound-less joy that flooded her senses. Nestling her head against his chest, Jessica listened for the re-assuring beat of Nick's heart and the steady, even rhythm of his breathing. *You came back to me,* she thought in ecstasy. *You came back.* Jessica closed her eyes, drowning in the sweet baby kisses Nick trailed across her forehead, down to her cheeks and over her earlobes, then along the slender curve of her neck.

"Nick . . . I thought you were . . ." Jessica's voice faltered.

Nick squeezed her tighter as if to silence her. "I'm here now. Everything's all right." Tenderly he brushed a strand of hair out of her eyes while the corners of his mouth suddenly drooped into a frown. "Where is he?"

"Gone . . ." Jessica barely breathed.

"How?"

"Overboard . . . ," she answered thickly, looking at the railing near the stern. "He was coming at me, but then he fell back and I got scared, so I hit him with—" Her voice breaking, she pointed at the malfunctioning dart gun.

Nick heaved a deep sigh and kissed her tem-ples. "It's all right, Jess. You did good."

Jessica's lashes were wet with tears. "He was just so crazy. . . ."

"I know. I found out when I got to the schooner."

"Katie?"

Nick swallowed hard. "Her real name was Katherine Horstmueller."

"*What?* You mean—"

"Eric was the kidnapper I've been trailing for some time now."

A terrible shudder rocked Jessica to the core. "He knew exactly who you were, didn't he? He planned this whole thing."

"Apparently," Nick answered somberly. "He killed Katherine when she didn't comply with his demands—I saw it all on videotape on the schooner. He had such a violent temper. . . . Oh, Jess, I was so scared something was going to happen to you."

Jessica rested her aching head on Nick's shoulder. "It all makes sense now."

"But I feel so terrible about everything— about leaving you behind, about botching the kidnapping sting. . . ." Nick paused to take a deep breath, his green eyes turning glassy. "That woman is dead because of my mistake—"

Jessica silenced Nick by pressing her warm, soft lips against his and lacing her arms around his neck. Nick responded passionately to her touch, his bittersweet kisses mingling with

Jessica's own relief and sadness. Their tired, broken bodies seemed to melt together as one, healed by the glow of their mutual, undying love.

"Everything is going to be all right, Nick, because we did the best we could," Jessica murmured in his ear. Her arms tightened around him, but she felt as if she could never get close enough.

Nick shook his head. "I didn't do enough—I should've been able to get Eric when I had the chance. . . ."

"Believe me, Eric paid dearly for what he did to her," Jessica assured him. Tilting back her head, she placed a gentle kiss on Nick's lower lip. "But he didn't get the best of us. We're together now, and we have to be strong," Jessica whispered. "The nightmare is finally over."

This is the life, Elizabeth thought with a languid smile as she collapsed into a chair on the deck of the *Halcyon* so she could soak up a few rays before they all got back to shore. Jessica and Nick were below deck fixing something to eat, as absorbed in each other as ever. Matt was just up ahead in the racer, towing the disabled yacht back to shore. And Elizabeth sat serenely in the sun after having changed into a pair of

Jessica's shorts and a clean T-shirt, happy that peace was once again restored in her tiny corner of the world.

It's so strange how things work out, Elizabeth mused as she slathered sunscreen on her arms and face. Elizabeth felt bad about falsely accusing Nick, but if she hadn't been so erroneously convinced that Nick was abusing Jessica, she would have never made the trip out to sea. And that could have spelled disaster. They would've never rescued Nick in time, Jessica might've been stranded alone out on the water for days, and of course, Elizabeth would've never had the chance to meet Matt.

Sometimes the most genuine mistakes produced the best results.

Elizabeth wiggled her bare toes in the sun and loosened her braid, letting her golden hair flow in the wind. Matt turned from *Midnight Blue's* steering wheel and gave her an amiable wave, looking as hopelessly gorgeous as ever. Feeling unusually brave, Elizabeth blew a kiss in his direction. Matt staggered backward jokingly, clutching at his heart.

As Elizabeth settled back and closed her eyes, a picture of Matt was printed indelibly on her brain. *Gorgeous, kind,* and *funny . . . this guy has it all.* As much as she hated to admit it, Elizabeth felt all the signs of an intense crush coming on.

She had trouble making eye contact with him, was overly self-conscious of every little movement she made, and had a heightened awareness of every look and gesture Matt made and every word he said. It was both maddening and exhilarating at the same time.

Maybe I'll ask him out when we get onshore, she thought. Clearly the enormous, cathartic release of stress had left Elizabeth's spirit feeling bubbly and daring. While the sun warmed her skin, Elizabeth indulged herself in a delicious daydream, imagining that she was sailing around the world with Matt. The sun was bright, and the water as warm and crystal blue as Matt's eyes. In between stops at exotic ports of call, Matt expertly sailed the racer while Elizabeth sunbathed and read fantastic books.

I can see it now, Elizabeth hummed in her meditative state. She was feeling giddy and indulgent—just like Jessica did twenty-four hours a day, she was sure. *I'm sitting here with my eyes closed, without a care in the world, and Matt suddenly looks over and is so taken by my beauty that he drops whatever he's doing and comes over to me.*

"Would you like a shoulder massage?" he asks.

I carefully put my book aside and smile. "Why, yes, Matt, that would be divine. . . ."

He places his strong hands on my shoulders and gently kneads the muscles between his fingers. . . .

The fantasy was so vivid, Elizabeth nearly sighed out loud. She swore she could almost feel Matt's hands working at her tense muscles, gradually pressing harder and harder. . . .

Elizabeth's eyes suddenly bolted open while the rest of her was completely frozen in place. *This is no dream*, she thought in silent alarm. *Someone is really massaging my shoulders.*

But it wasn't Matt—he was busy steering the racer up ahead. *And Nick—how could it be Nick*, she wondered, *unless he's mistaken me for Jessica?* That seemed beyond doubtful in Elizabeth's mind—Nick and Jessica had hardly left each other's side since the reunion.

Elizabeth gripped the arms of the deck chair as the strong, invisible thumbs dug deeper and deeper into her shoulders. "Ouch," she complained. "That's too hard." She sat up a little and noticed out of the corner of her eye a thin trail of bright red blood snaking down her arm.

"What—?" She jolted fully awake with a start. There was no denying it. The blood was virtually coursing down her body now.

"Get away from me!" Elizabeth screamed, but as she tried to pull herself away, the hands encircled her throat, squeezing tighter and tighter. Her gaze darted over and found Matt,

228

who had returned to helming *Midnight Blue* with his back toward her, completely oblivious to the attack. She tried to yell his name, but the words were caught in her throat, cut off by the strong, masculine hands that were threatening to crush her slender neck. All that escaped from her lips was a tiny, breathless gasp.

Then everything went black.

Chapter
Seventeen

"Do you think it's too late to salvage our vacation?" Jessica asked, taking a can of chicken soup from the galley cupboard. "We still have a few hours before we get to shore."

Nick gracefully swept her up in his arms and gently tilted her back in a romantic dip. "I can think of a few ways we can make up for it," he said, kissing her seductively.

Jessica giggled. "I was thinking it might be fun if we—" She suddenly stopped, and a strange look came over her face. "Did you hear that?"

Nick was too intoxicated by the honey scent of Jessica's hair to notice much else. He lazily nibbled at her earlobe. "Hear what?"

Jessica bolted upright, pulling away from him. "Listen."

Standing still, Nick obeyed, but all he heard was the lapping waves hitting the side of the boat. Silently he wondered if Jessica was experiencing some posttraumatic paranoia. "I don't hear anything out of the ordinary."

Deep furrows appeared above her brow. "I know I heard something," she said, shaking her head. "I think it's Liz. I'd better go up on deck and make sure everything's all right." She headed for the stairs.

"Go ahead," Nick encouraged, sighing inwardly. It had been a long, difficult trip—all he wanted now was a little time alone with Jessica without too many interruptions, but he wasn't about to complain this time. If the events of the last twenty-four hours had taught him anything at all, it was that every living moment he had was a gift—he'd take whatever he could get.

Peeking her head out at the top of the stairs, Jessica raced back down, her face as white as a sheet. "He's back, Nick!" she cried in hysteria.

"Calm down, Jess. What are you—"

"I don't know how, but he's back! He's back, and he's got Elizabeth!"

Nick's blood froze. "Eric?"

Jessica grabbed Nick's wrist and yanked him toward the stairs. "Hurry! He's going to kill her!"

"Stay down here!" Without a second's

hesitation Nick bounded up the stairs two at a time. What he witnessed on deck was straight out of a horror movie. Eric was at the other end of the deck with his back turned, blood leaking from his gaping head wound and trickling down his back in jagged patterns like lines on a gruesome map. His throbbing, muscular arms were bowed on either side of him, blue veins bulging, and his violent hands were locked around Elizabeth's neck in a death grip. Her head shook limply back and forth like a rag doll's as he strangled her, a grisly bubbling sound coming from her throat.

Nick clenched his fists into a tight ball, every nerve in his body surging with trepidation. *What can I do?* he wondered, his mind spinning wildly as he tried to plot his next move. Nick's brain commanded his body to race to Elizabeth's aid, but his feet remained firmly in place, crippled by the memory of the botched kidnapping.

Suddenly Nick was back at the pickup site, watching Vincent Horstmueller from an unmarked van as he walked to the huge stone fountain in the middle of the city park, carrying a metal briefcase containing the ransom. Nick remembered every nerve-jangling second—the anxious, painful moments waiting inside the van, his service revolver gripped with both hands, poised just above his ear . . . the beads of sweat that trickled down the sides of his face . . . the quickening of his pulse, the shallow sound of his own breathing. But most of all Nick recalled the burning, suffocating heat that rose from his collar every time he worried that the kidnapper was going to get the money and run without releasing Katherine. The next thing Nick remembered, he was jumping out of the van and running toward the masked kidnapper, gun aimed right at his head.

And that's when I blew it, Nick recalled. Eric had stared fearlessly into Nick's eyes and run, pulling a stumbling Katherine along behind him. There was no way Nick could have made the shot without hitting her. All he could do was stand there, his finger frozen on the trigger, while the kidnapper escaped with his hostage.

As precious seconds ticked away, Nick broke out into a cold sweat. Elizabeth's arms were dangling limply on either side of the chair.

Confront your fear, Fox . . . you're not going to get another chance. . . .

Nick tried to swallow, but he felt himself choking. He knew he was no match for Eric's nearly superhuman strength. The only advantage he'd have would be to take Eric by surprise.

Do it, urged a strong inner voice. *Do it for Elizabeth . . . for everything he put Jessica through. . . . Do it for Katherine Horstmueller. You owe her that much.*

With one foot in front of the other, Nick inhaled deeply and slowly approached Eric from behind, silently padding across the deck. As Nick focused on the matted, bloodied back of Eric's head the crippling fear began to fall away, replaced by a rage that was slowly building inside him like a tidal wave. The overwhelming pressure rose higher and higher, overtaking Nick, speeding out of control. His eyes burned like coals in his skull. *It's payback time, Eric,* Nick thought, feeling the cresting wave of adrenaline pounding through his extremities. *This time you're going down.*

Then, like a tightly coiled spring suddenly releasing, Nick rushed Eric and with one smooth motion hooked his arms through Eric's, trying with all his strength to pull them back.

Eric laughed as casually as if they were playing a friendly game of arm wrestling. He turned his head to the side to try to see who had jumped him. "Fox, is that you? What a surprise," he answered, still gripping

235

Elizabeth in his iron fists. "I never would've believed you were clever enough to find your way back here. I'm terribly disappointed in you."

Eric suddenly pulled his arms forward in a powerful stroke, dragging Nick with him. Nick's face smacked against Eric's back as he tried to regain control, the stench of dried blood filling his nostrils. "Let go of her," he hissed through clenched teeth, straining futilely against Eric's arms. "Leave her out of this. Let's just make it you and me. One-on-one."

"Good idea, Fox. It's something I've been looking forward to for a long time." Eric released Elizabeth, who slumped lifelessly in the deck chair. "I think I'm done with Jessica anyway. She was a very bad girl while you were gone, Fox. I don't think you would've been pleased." Eric's scratched and bruised face suddenly turned as hard as raw steel as he looked down at the unconscious Wakefield twin he'd obviously mistaken for Jessica. With lightning bolt speed, he wrapped his ankle around one of the wooden legs of the chair and kicked it up into the air with a sweep, knocking it and Elizabeth onto the deck.

Elizabeth didn't move at all; the side of her bruised face and neck were pressed against the deck. Her white T-shirt was stained with blood.

It was hard to tell if the blood was her own or Eric's.

You animal, Nick thought in disgust, stunned by the sheer, pointless brutality of Eric's actions. *There's no way I'm letting you get away this time. You can bet on it.*

While Nick's insides quivered like jelly, he forced himself to remain hard and confrontational on the exterior. Eric was a psychotic who played as if he had nothing to lose, and Nick needed every possible advantage he could find, even the most superficial ones.

Nick's gaze locked onto Eric's threateningly as they circled each other like panthers, each assessing the situation and getting a feel for the turf, their muscles poised and ready for action. Eric raised one dark, haughty eyebrow, as if he found the current circumstances incredibly amusing. Nick bared his teeth like a dog ready to attack.

The question that had been burning inside Nick ever since he'd discovered the truth about Eric on the schooner suddenly bubbled to the surface. He found himself unable to hold it back. "Why did you murder Katherine Horstmueller?" he spat angrily, the veins popping out of his neck.

Eric grinned, obviously pleased with himself. "Good for you, Fox. You found the little surprise I left for you on the schooner."

"That and the initials you carved into the hull."

"Oh, my." Eric chuckled. "I'm *so* impressed. Since you made it that far, I wonder if you had a chance to watch the little video I made of Miss Horstmueller's final moments. I didn't intend to record the event for posterity, of course. But the little witch just wouldn't cooperate."

Nick's throat closed up at the memory. "You didn't have to kill her," he insisted solemnly.

"I didn't kill her, Fox. *You* killed her."

"No, I didn't," Nick swore, the anxiety within him building up to near breaking point.

"Yes, you did, by botching the pickup." Eric's eyes gleamed like a snake's. "If you hadn't gotten involved, I would've let her go, and everything would've been just fine."

Nick flinched. Eric had found the exact nerve to touch and then pounced on it savagely. But Nick's response to Eric's taunt came in the form of a blazing rage that only helped to fuel the vengeful fire burning within him. Suddenly he felt stronger and more confident than ever.

"If you think you were punishing me by murdering her, Eric, you're wrong." Nick rocked back and forth on his heels cockily, prepared for any other tricks Eric might be keeping under his sleeves. "It's backfiring on you. They're going to put you away for life."

Eric's upper lip curled in a scornful sneer. "Those bunch of amateurs you call a police department? They wouldn't see me if I was right under their noses."

Anger flared inside Nick's guts, urging him to throw a sucker punch. But Nick held back, remaining cool and calm on the outside. Nick only fought dirty when pushed beyond the limit; Eric hadn't quite pushed him there yet. "I got close, believe me," Nick bragged. "It wouldn't take them that long to get you."

"You're the best they've got, Fox—and that's not saying much." Eric threw back his head and laughed. He bounced on his heels, his fists jabbing at the air. The pace was quickening. "You have pretty good tracking instincts, but mine are far superior to yours or anyone's in that entire lame precinct, for that matter. I could outrun you any day."

"I doubt that," Nick scoffed. He held his arms up in front of him in a boxer's stance.

"I called your office two days ago. . . ." Eric lunged frenetically from side to side, throwing unpredictable punches from the left to the right, seemingly enjoying watching Nick flinch. "Those boneheads at the precinct told me you were out to sea. Can you believe that? Just giving out information to whoever asks for it?"

Nick's shoulders slumped a fraction of an inch as he felt his psychological edge slipping. *Don't let him get to you,* he told himself. *Eric's a liar, a kidnapper, and a vicious murderer. He wants to break you down. Don't give him the satisfaction.*

"I went to every yacht rental place in the area, figuring a second-rate detective like yourself couldn't afford one of your own," Eric continued gleefully. He threw a solid punch directly at Nick's face; Nick dodged it at the last second, but he felt Eric's bloody knuckle graze his cheek. "You see, I knew exactly how to find you when I needed to. Unlike you, I'm not about to let my prey slip through my fingers."

I'll never beat this guy, Nick thought, psyching himself out against his will. *He's going to kill me, then Elizabeth and Jessica too.* Nick's heart was beating so furiously, it felt as if it were about to plow right through his rib cage. "Surrender right now, Eric, and I promise I'll talk to the prosecutor. They can go easy on you."

"What? Walk away from a fight I'm going to win? I have another idea." With explosive force Eric burst forth with an uppercut that landed

240

right under Nick's chin, forcing his head to ricochet back and forth brutally.

Groaning, Nick dropped to his knees, feeling as if he could never walk again. But the vision of Jessica hiding terrified under the deck forced him to get up on his feet once again. "Is that the best you can do?" he snarled.

"All right!" Eric cheered. "You know, Fox, I have to say that that was one great idea of yours. Let's battle it out, one-on-one, just like you said. If I win, you let me go. If you win, I'll let you live."

Nick's entire head throbbed with white-hot pain, and his vision had blurred from the blow to the jaw. He shook his head, sending shock waves of pain through his spine with every inch he moved. "No deal, Griffin. Either way you're going to jai—"

"Win!" Eric interrupted cheerfully. "Either way I'm going to win. You're so right, Officer."

Eric drew back his arm with the tension of a crossbow, then mercilessly released it. Nick managed to throw up his hands and shield his face, deflecting Eric's nuclear-strength blow. But in the process Nick had brought up both arms near his head, leaving his torso wide open. Eric took full advantage of the opportunity, socking him in the solar plexus. Doubling over in excruciating pain, Nick

241

wheezed, trying desperately to fill his lungs with air.

Eric paused, apparently waiting for Nick to recover before doing even more damage to him. "It can't be over already!" Eric whined sarcastically, rubbing the palms of his hands together. "We've hardly even gotten warmed up! Come on, Fox, don't go and disappoint me even more."

Nick's lungs burned for air. He still hadn't completely recovered from nearly drowning the horrific night before in the schooner, and what little strength and energy he had left were now rapidly draining away to nothing. A sour sickness churned in the pit of Nick's stomach and radiated throughout the rest of his body, which was pleading with Nick to surrender. But Nick's mind wouldn't let him give up—not on his life, or Jessica's, or anyone else's.

This man killed Katherine Horstmueller, he reminded himself.

This man tried to kill you.

This man tried to take Jessica away.

He could still kill her, if given a chance. . . .

That last thought filled Nick with renewed strength and caused vengeful blood to flow through his veins. With a ferocious roar Nick charged at Eric like a bull. Slamming the top of his head into Eric's chest and throwing all his weight against him, Nick violently shoved Eric back several feet into the boat's steering wheel.

Eric groaned in pain. "Think you're a tough guy?" he asked, grasping Nick's hair with one hand. With a loud, *"Kiaii!"* Eric pulled Nick's head back and landed a sharp, solid punch right on the bridge of his nose.

White and blue sparks flashed behind Nick's eyes as he stumbled backward, his vision clouded and blurry. Eric brought his fist down on him again, this time in the mouth. Nick's lips were crushed back against his teeth, causing an agonizing jolt of painful lightning to streak through his brain. A trickle of blood seeped out the corner of his mouth, and his teeth hurt so badly, they itched.

I can't hang on much longer, Nick thought between labored, raspy breaths. Nothing in all his years of police training had prepared him for an assault like this. Every part of his head ached—his nose, his chin, even his entire skull throbbed and swelled. The metallic taste of blood oozed in his mouth and covered his tongue like sickly, stained velvet.

"You've made this much too easy," Eric panted. He took in a deep breath, effortlessly lifting his right leg and cocking his knee back to his chest. He held his leg there at waist level with the perfect skill and balance that came only with long hours of disciplined martial arts training.

Knowing what was coming, Nick backed away, cowering with fear and pain. "No . . . please don't," he whimpered, feeling the blood from his mouth drip down off his bruised chin. He stared at Eric's outstretched leg through half-closed, swollen eyes and began to shake with terror. He had to give up now—for the twins' sake. If Eric knocked him out, there was no telling what he might do while he was unconscious. "I surrender," Nick said quietly, ashamedly. "I'll let you go—"

"Why would I want to stop now?" Eric asked matter-of-factly, bringing down his leg and bouncing on the balls of his feet like a fighter warming up before a match. "I mean, I'm having too much fun. I've got you right where I want you now. No way am I letting you go." Grinning, Eric jumped up and his entire body whirled around in a powerful spiral, spinning through the air like a tornado.

Racked with pain, Nick could hardly move. All he could do was watch as Eric's leg swung over Nick's shoulder and slammed mercilessly against his neck, the pain detonating inside him like an atomic bomb.

* * *

"I can't take this anymore!" Jessica shouted tensely. She'd been pacing the galley endlessly, listening to the commotion up above, helplessly wondering what was happening. *Is Liz OK? Did Nick hold him off? What's happening?* The questions spun like a top in her mind, threatening to drive her insane.

"I don't care what Nick says. I'm going up there now." Jessica raced up the stairs. *Why did I ever agree to stay down here?* she wondered. *He needs my help.* After all, she was the one who'd spent hours alone with that maniac—she had more than a few ideas how to keep him in line. No one could fight him alone; the only reason Jessica defeated him the first time around was because she had a raging storm to back her up. She'd even thought she'd killed him then. How wrong she was!

Panic swelled inside Jessica's heart, causing it to beat unnaturally quickly. *Does Nick have any idea what he's getting himself into?* she wondered, remembering the horror at seeing Eric's bloody face again so soon after she'd imagined him dead.

Once Jessica made it to the door, she had to stifle a cry. Nick was lying on the ground, grimacing in agony, his face bloodied and swollen. Elizabeth was a few feet away, lying motionless, her shirt soaked in blood. Jessica was relieved to see they were still breathing, but Eric was prowling around them both like a cheetah ready to devour its prey.

What has that beast done to them? Jessica wondered, bursting into silent tears, covering her mouth to hold back her hysterical screams. Suddenly Eric looked up, and she caught her breath, afraid he'd heard her. But when he turned toward the bow, Jessica assumed he was checking to make sure that Matt hadn't noticed anything transpiring from his place behind the wheel of *Midnight Blue*. Judging from the way the yacht was coasting along at a healthy clip, their friendly towboat driver was blissfully unaware of it all.

Stay calm, Jessica told herself between short, erratic breaths. *Don't do anything to draw his attention. Now think. There has to be something you can do to distract him.* She hunkered down into the stairway and watched, her mind whirling.

"You said you'd let me live," Nick murmured groggily. The raspy, pained breaks in his voice ripped Jessica's heart to shreds. "That was part of the deal."

"I've changed the rules." Eric reached down and picked up something. Jessica squinted into the sun, trying to make out what it was. A moment later Jessica recognized the object only too well. It was the dart gun.

"They're going to track you down, no matter what," Nick said almost pleadingly. "I can make things easy on you."

Eric lowered the barrel of the dart gun and aimed it right between Nick's eyes at point-blank range. "And why should I trust you, Fox? Even if you were being honest, *which I highly doubt,* you'd probably just mess it all up, the same way you do everything else."

Jessica squirmed in unbearable anguish. Even though she knew the dart gun didn't work, she still couldn't allow herself to relax. *Doesn't Eric remember how the gun misfired when I tried to use it?* she wondered. *Or is he just trying to scare Nick to death?* Being the sick, twisted guy Eric was, she was tempted to believe the latter. Jessica leaned forward, biting her knuckles to keep from screaming. *The gun isn't going to work. . . . He knows that. . . . Nick will be fine. . . .*

No sooner had Jessica thought that Nick would be safe when Eric, grinning evilly, delicately placed his index finger on a tiny lever near the gun's trigger and flipped it with a flourish.

The safety release.

Oh no! Jessica cried internally. *That's why it didn't work when I tried to use it! The gun isn't broken—it works just fine!*

With every breath Jessica took, she felt a stabbing pain in her chest. "This isn't a joke,"

Jessica whispered under her breath. "Eric's going to kill Nick. He's really going to do it this time. And there's nothing I can do about it!"

"Go ahead! Finish me off!" Nick shouted, spitting in Eric's face. "I hope you rot in hell!"

Eric leveled the gun right between Nick's eyes. "Then I'll be seeing you there, Fox. Any last words?"

Chapter
Eighteen

"Eric, wait!"

Eric looked up from the gun and turned his head in the direction of the bell-toned voice. As if she were a mirage, there, standing by the stairs to the cabin, was Jessica. Yes—she must be a mirage! She stared at him with clear, alert eyes, showing no signs of being knocked out at all. And when she began walking toward him, her T-shirt clean and sparkling white, her incomparably beautiful blond hair floated in the wind like a golden sanctuary.

"Jessica?" Eric asked, unable to rid his voice of confusion. "Jessica, is that you?"

"Yes, Eric, I'm right here," she answered coolly, moving closer still.

"But . . ." Eric turned to the blood-covered body at the other end of the deck. *That's her. . . . I know it is. . . . But how could she be in two places at once?* He rubbed his eyes and looked again. The same hair, the same face, the same clothes . . . *Am I going crazy?*

"I thought you were over there," he said, pointing to the other blond woman who lay crumpled on the deck.

Jessica nodded. Her face was pale white. "Yes, Eric. I *am* over there . . . and I'm here too."

"That's impossible—"

"No, it's not," Jessica answered, moving ever closer, her hips swaying seductively.

Eric started inching away from her. "What do you mean?" he demanded, his voice taking on a frightened edge. The gun trembled in his hands. "What's that over there?"

Jessica's eyes turned cold. "It's my dead body, Eric. You may have killed me physically, but you can't kill my spirit," she whispered hauntingly. "I'm here to see that you pay for your crime." She reached out to touch his arm, but Eric jumped back.

"Don't touch me!" he cried. "You're not a ghost—are you? Is this some kind of weird joke?"

"Hardly," Jessica answered, her voice deadly serious. "It's time to pay your dues. I hope you're prepared."

Eric's knees trembled uncontrollably as he

backed away, turning to check on Nick. He was staring up at the two of them, his jaw hanging open in disbelief. Eric whirled around, almost expecting to see that Jessica had vanished. But she was still there, smiling eerily at him. "Prove it," he challenged, his voice quavering.

Jessica stopped. "What do you mean?"

"If you're a real ghost, then prove it," Eric repeated. His head ached and he felt dizzy, as if his equilibrium was off. "If you're what you say you are, then nothing can hurt you, right?"

"Right," Jessica answered after a brief pause.

Eric lifted the gun and aimed it straight at her, his hands shaking to keep it steady. "So let's see what happens when I drive this dart right through your head."

Fear stabbed deeply into Nick's heart as he watched the events unfolding above him. Eric had completely moved his attention from Nick and was now focused on Jessica, aiming the gun right in her face.

Why didn't you stay below deck like I asked you to, Jessica? he asked silently. *Why did you have to go and put yourself in danger?*

An air of tragic doom was descending all around him, and Nick felt its chill right down to his marrow. There wasn't going to be a happy ending after all.

"Go right ahead—give me your best shot!" Jessica egged him on, moving even closer to the barrel of the gun.

Don't, Jess, this is no time to call his bluff. . . .

As Eric's finger curled around the trigger Nick felt his stomach caving in. "No!" he shouted, suddenly throwing his arms over his head and grabbing at Eric's ankles. Caught off guard, Eric wobbled a bit, struggling to regain his balance.

"Get off me!" Eric cried, swinging the gun perilously close to Nick's head.

Grunting in pain, Nick hugged Eric's ankles with one arm, then punched the back of his knees with the other. Eric's legs folded almost instantly, sending him to the floor with a crash. Eric's arms and fingers splayed out in front of him in an attempt to break his fall, the gun dropping out of his hands. As the butt of the gun slammed against the deck a dart suddenly discharged, just grazing the side of Jessica's leg, leaving a blazing red scratch in its wake.

"Watch it, Nick!" Jessica screamed as the two men lay side by side on the yacht's deck. Eric crawled a few inches and reached for the dart gun, but Jessica stepped on his fingers before he could touch it.

"Dumb witch!" Eric howled in pain.

Jessica shot him a nasty look, and with a

graceful, satisfying kick she sent the dart gun scuttling off the edge of the deck into the water.

"Get out of the way, Jessica!" Nick called hoarsely, trying to sit up.

"No—I want to help!"

"Go see if your sister's all right!" he shouted, not taking his swollen eyes off of Eric for even a moment. Gritting his teeth, Nick braced himself to do battle again.

"Sister!" Eric's venomous eyes glared at Nick, his skin reddening like coals on a fire at the realization that he'd been had. His chest rose and fell in heavy breaths as he got to his knees. "Ready for round two?"

"Why don't you just throw yourself overboard?" Nick snapped. It was sapping all his will just to keep himself upright. He leaned forward with his fists in front of him, trying desperately to ignore the hot, shooting pain that started from his neck and branched like lightning down his back. "Maybe I'll do it for you. It's over, Griffin. Let's call it even!"

"It'll never be over, Fox, as long as you're around," Eric snarled. The gash in the back of his head was still flowing, but he seemed as alert as ever, strangely unfazed by the loss of blood. "I won't be happy until you're in the grave."

"Then I guess you're not going to be happy for a long, long time," Nick replied. Up until that moment he hadn't been out for blood—his only purpose for fighting was to restrain Eric. But suddenly it dawned on him that for Eric it was a matter of pride that could only be resolved with a fight to the death. For Nick it was nothing more than pure survival.

Just when he thought he didn't have the strength to fight anymore, Nick's body started taking over where his mind was failing him, pumping him full of pain-numbing adrenaline. His senses heightened, and the sluggishness began to wear off. *This is it, Fox,* he told himself as he faced down his maniacal opponent. *You'd better make this one count.* Nick was running on borrowed energy, with just enough fuel to make it through the next few moments. His fragile body was like a condemned building on the verge of collapse—one wrong move, and it could cost him his life.

"I'll give you one to start, just to make things a little more even," Eric said, holding his hands up in the air. "Let's see what you can do."

Nick didn't hesitate for a second, taking the opportunity to nail Eric with a right hook to the jaw. Eric's eyes widened in surprise and he fell back a little. Before Eric had a chance to recover, Nick slammed his left fist across the other side of Eric's face, throwing his entire weight behind it. Half a second later Nick jabbed again, left, then right, gaining speed and momentum, pummeling Eric's face until he fell flat on his back.

The tide had turned. Nick had him pinned to the ground and Eric was shielding his face from the punches, completely restrained—just where Nick had wanted him.

"Stop!" Eric finally cried in surrender.

But Nick couldn't stop. He didn't *want* to. His fists were flying through the air with gleeful fury, pounding out every fear and trauma that he had experienced on the schooner. He was taking revenge for the hell Eric had put Jessica through, for attacking Elizabeth, and for ending Katherine Horstmueller's life. He wanted Eric to pay dearly for all the damage he had done.

But as Nick's frenzied punches slowed and his body grew tired, he began slowly to realize that he was no better than Eric. In a matter of seconds he had crossed that invisible line between fighting for survival and fighting for the pleasure of violence.

I'm acting like an animal, Nick thought with shame, his fist poised in the air inches above Eric's battered face. The murderer's glazed eyes stared up at him vacantly, waiting in surrender for the next blow. *What am I doing?* Nick thought. *I don't want to be a psycho—*

No sooner had Nick dropped his fists at his sides and started to move away than Eric sprang up and tackled him to the floor. Completely taken off guard, Nick suddenly found himself facedown against the deck floor, his arms pinned to his sides, completely immobilized. He kicked his legs wildly, but it didn't help at all. Nick was totally at Eric's mercy.

"This is no good," Eric growled, his voice as rough as the serrated edge of a hunting knife. As fast as quicksilver he rolled Nick onto his back and straddled him, pinning Nick's arms down with his knees.

Nick's head was hanging back off the edge of the deck, his ears filling with the sounds of rushing water just below him. Drops of Eric's blood were falling down on his face, each drop resonating like the tick of a clock's second hand as it counted down the seconds until Nick met his doom.

It's finally come to this, Nick thought sadly, hoping that Jessica wasn't watching. *I love you, Jessica; I always will. . . .* Nick closed his eyes in helpless surrender, praying that he wouldn't suffer too much longer.

"That's better," Eric said as his crushing hands encircled Nick's throat. "I want to see the look on your face when you die."

*   *   *

Sunlight entered Elizabeth's consciousness as if a butcher knife had just split her skull in two. Blearily she stared up at Jessica, who sat hovering over her with a wild look in her blue-green eyes.

"Are you all right, Liz?" she said urgently, patting her gently on the face.

Elizabeth drew in a sharp, painful breath, the air irritating her tender throat. She rolled groggily from side to side, trying to remember what had happened before she blacked out. "I was just sitting there," Elizabeth whispered, touching the sore areas on her neck. "And someone came up behind me—"

"It was Eric, the psycho," Jessica interrupted, her voice rising an octave. "I don't know how he did it, but he's back . . . and he's fighting with Nick." Jessica jumped to her feet, her eyes darting all over the deck as if she were looking for a weapon or something. She was wringing her hands nervously, frightened tears dotting her cheeks. "I'm afraid he's going to *kill* him!"

As Elizabeth's vision cleared she looked around the fallen deck chair next to her and saw Eric's bloody back leaning over Nick, who was kicking his legs like mad. Eric had him by the throat—just like he'd had her, but Nick's head was actually hanging off the deck, his shoulders edging perilously toward the water. Elizabeth choked back a cry as she remembered the scalding pain and the horrific panic she felt as her throat began closing in on her. Seeing Nick going through the same thing was like living every terrifying moment all over again.

We have to stop him, she thought, stumbling to her feet. *There has to be something we can do.* . . .

Elizabeth spotted the back of Matt's head in the racer. He was facing forward, seemingly unaware that anything had happened at all. "Matt!" she cried at the top of her lungs, but he didn't turn around. "Matt! Over here!"

Jessica yelled with her a few times, but their voices wouldn't carry above the din of the racer's engine. "He can't hear us. . . . I don't think he could get up here anyway. . . ." Deep worry lines creased Jessica's face. She looked as if she was about to crack at any minute.

On the other side of the deck Eric was choking Nick so hard, his arms were shaking. Elizabeth's stomach soured as she watched Nick's hands flailing helplessly in the air, swinging blindly at Eric, then struggling to pry his fingers off his throat. Jessica was yanking at the railing in an apparent attempt to pull off a section to use as a weapon, but to no avail.

"Think of something, Liz!" Jessica cried,

beating her fists furiously against the railing. "Hurry!"

At the exact same moment her sister's pleading cries reached her ears, Elizabeth spotted something they had completely overlooked. The one thing that had practically been staring them in the face all along.

The deck chair.

Of course, Elizabeth thought, grasping onto her last silver thread of hope. *Why didn't I see this before?*

Jessica didn't even ask—she already knew what her sister had in mind. It was one of those instances where they were able to communicate without a single word, look, or gesture—just a simple thought that seemed to travel through the air from one twin to the other. Silently the plan was set in motion, and Jessica already knew her part.

I hope this works, Jessica tried to silently communicate to her sister. *We don't have much choice* was her second thought, almost as if Elizabeth had answered her herself.

While Elizabeth reached for the deck chair, Jessica went into action. "Eric," she called sweetly, standing to the right of him. "Eric, darling, please look over here."

Eric didn't answer. He just kept brutally

shaking Nick, whose eyes were starting to roll back in his head.

"Eric!" Jessica yelled, more urgently this time. Elizabeth was silently approaching him from the left, holding fast to the wooden legs of the chair. "There's something I want to show you."

"Leave me alone, you little tramp!" Eric snarled. "You've made a fool out of me for the last time."

Jessica's blood pressure was rising. She walked toward Eric, averting her eyes from Nick's slackened body, plastering an apologetic smile on her face. "That's what I wanted to tell you—I'm sorry for what I did to you. I want to show you how sorry I am." She crouched down beside him and touched his shoulder, still sticky with blood.

Just beyond Eric, Jessica could see Elizabeth approaching stealthily with the deck chair poised high over her head. *I have to keep his attention,* Jessica thought, her mind reeling with nervous anticipation. She felt as if she were on a high wire, teetering on the brink of insanity. *Keep him looking this way. . . .*

Eric turned his head slightly in Jessica's direction, giving her a full view of the puffy black bruises swelling around his eyes and the blood streaming from his broken nose. He didn't let go of Nick.

"I don't believe you," he sneered. "Get out of my face."

Elizabeth was only a few feet away. Nick was obviously in dangerous need of air, and they were moments away from pulling off their scheme. But now Jessica knew that the outcome depended fully and entirely on her. All their lives were in her hands.

"I'm serious," Jessica said in a silken voice. "Nick means nothing to me."

"Liar," Eric spat. He didn't let go.

Elizabeth was only inches away, her arms shaking from the strain of the heavy chair above her head. Jessica could tell by the way her lips were drawn tightly against her teeth that Elizabeth couldn't hang on much longer.

Do something crazy, a voice in her head urged. *Do something drastic. Something that will take him completely by surprise.* Although the simple idea of it sent a violent wave of nausea charging toward Jessica's very core, she knew immediately what she had to do. *Remember, this is for Nick. You'd do anything to save Nick. Nick will understand.*

"Hey, Eric," Jessica called softly. "Please— look at me."

Eric didn't respond. Inhaling deeply, Jessica slipped her left arm around Eric's damp neck and, gently touching his chin, she turned his beastly face toward hers. This time he didn't fight.

Out of the corner of her eye Jessica saw Eric slowly release his grip. "You've been fighting so hard," she said, staring deeply into his cold, black eyes. "Why don't you take a little break?"

Eric nodded almost imperceptibly at Jessica, totally entranced by her, his purple lips parting in expectation. Eric's lips were a violent contrast to Elizabeth's beet red face, which hovered right behind him. The deck chair was still poised above Elizabeth's head shakily, as if she was waiting for the perfect moment to reveal itself.

With a seductive look Jessica pulled Eric close to her, knowing it was her last resort. Closing her eyes, she pressed her soft lips against his, revulsion bubbling up inside her. Eric responded passionately, running his murderous hands through her hair.

Just pretend it's Nick, Jessica told herself, trying to ward off the continuous waves of disgust and horror that kept hitting her again and again without mercy. Thankfully Nick suddenly stirred, brushing his arm listlessly against her leg.

He's conscious! Jessica realized, her relief almost eclipsed by regret as Eric's mouth explored hers. *I'm so sorry you have to see this, Nick—please forgive me. . . .* A moment later

Jessica felt the soft tap of Nick's fingers on her knee, reassuring her that he understood.

Jessica pulled away as quickly as she could without arousing suspicion. "Wow," she breathed seductively as she leaned back out of harm's way. "You have no idea how long I've been waiting for this, Eric."

Just as Eric reached out for more, Elizabeth's arms swung into motion. She slammed the heavy wooden deck chair against his back while Jessica shielded her face from the flying splinters. For one seemingly endless moment Jessica watched breathlessly as Eric wobbled, staring blankly at her. He started to get up, his eyes wet and glassy, but then he suddenly keeled over, falling unconscious at her feet.

Chapter
Nineteen

"We'd better do something about Eric," Elizabeth said worriedly, poking his arm with the toe of her sneaker. "Who knows how long he'll be out."

"There's some rope in the closet downstairs," Jessica said, tending to Nick's fresh wounds. "We should probably tie him up."

Elizabeth headed for the stairs. "It'd probably take steel cable to hold that guy."

It probably would, Nick thought ruefully, glancing over at Eric's body for the five-hundredth time to assure himself it wasn't moving. Lying with his head on Jessica's lap, Nick basked in the lavish attention she was giving him, cleaning his wounds with a damp cloth, bandaging his cuts and bruises. Closing his eyes, Nick imagined himself as a wounded soldier on the battlefield and Jessica as

265

the beautiful, dedicated nurse who saved his life.

Gently Jessica tilted Nick's head back to look at the cut underneath his chin, and he winced from the sudden sharp pain in his neck. Jessica groaned in sympathy. "I can't believe he did this to you," she said quietly.

"Neither can I," Nick murmured, meaning even more than Jessica probably realized. Of all the terrible things Eric had done to him—tricking him into going on the schooner, leaving him for dead, attacking him and nearly strangling him to death—the one thing that Nick absolutely couldn't get out of his mind was the memory of watching him kiss Jessica. Intellectually Nick understood why she had to do it, but knowing that certainly didn't make it any easier on his heart.

The incident had happened only a few moments ago, and already Nick had run through it a million times in his head. *Why did she have to kiss him for so long? Why couldn't she have just given him a quick peck on the cheek or something like that?* Nick tried to be objective about it, knowing consciously how ridiculous his questions were, but that didn't stop them from racing around in his mind. What it all boiled down to was that Jessica had been convincing. Too convincing.

Nick tried to curb the green monster inside him, but after several attempts at trying to bite his jealous tongue, he couldn't hold back any longer. "What was it like?" he suddenly asked.

Jessica looked down at him, her eyes narrowing. "What?"

"You know," Nick answered almost shyly, lowering his voice. "Kissing Eric."

"What do you mean, *what was it like?*"

Nick shrugged boyishly, aware that he had just entered very dangerous territory. "You know . . ."

Jessica threw down the towel. "You mean, did I *enjoy* it?"

Nick nodded lamely.

"It was one of the most horrifying experiences of my life," Jessica shouted, her voice tinged with outrage. "How on earth could you ask me such a question?"

"I just wanted to be sure, that's all." Nick sat up but kept his head lowered. "You looked like you might've liked it a little bit."

Jessica's upper lip curled in disgust. "I'm sorry you had to witness that, Nick, but may I remind you that I kissed that horrible man in order to save your life?"

"I know." Nick suddenly felt ashamed for ever bringing it up. "Sorry."

Jessica fell quiet for a moment. "I'm really confused, Nick. I thought you were OK with it."

"What made you think that?"

"The way you tapped me on the knee while we were kissing," Jessica said, taking his hand to demonstrate. "You were trying to tell me that it was OK—you understood."

Nick shook his head. "I was trying to tell you to come up for air. I thought that kiss would never end."

"Oh . . ." Jessica started to laugh. "If it makes you feel any better, I was thinking of you the whole time."

"Yeah?" Nick grinned a little. "Does he kiss like me?"

"I'm not telling . . . ," Jessica teased. She slapped Nick playfully on the wrist, the one place left on his body that wasn't bruised or bleeding.

Elizabeth suddenly appeared with the rope, breaking the moment between them. "I tried to get Matt's attention, but he's completely absorbed in driving the boat. I don't think he has a clue what happened over here."

"He'll be in for a big surprise," Jessica mused. When Elizabeth headed for the far side of the yacht, Jessica caught Nick's eye for a long moment, smiling. He leaned in close, closer, waiting to feel her soft lips on his once again. . . .

"Hey, Nick?" Elizabeth called.

Nick groaned. "Yeah?" he asked, turning his

head away momentarily, missing the kiss.

"Sorry about what I said earlier." Elizabeth smiled wearily. "I was just a little stressed out."

Nick remembered Elizabeth's reaction when he'd first told her Jessica was alone on the yacht with Eric. Even though she'd yelled at him, Nick knew she had every right to do it.

"It's all right, Liz," Nick answered with a smile. "No hard feelings."

Jessica raised her eyebrows, her curiosity obviously piqued. "What is she talking about?"

"Nothing," Nick answered casually, sitting up with Jessica's help. His muscles were so achy and tired, they seemed to have absolutely no desire to work on their own. "Can you help me over to the radio?" he asked. "I want to notify the precinct so we can have some officers waiting when we reach the marina."

"It doesn't work," Jessica said, watching Elizabeth tie Eric's limp hands behind his back. "He ripped out the wires."

"Maybe I can patch them together," Nick said. He leaned against Jessica with his arm wrapped around her shoulders, amazed at how good it felt to be in the safety of Jessica's arms again.

It's over, Nick told himself, unable to hold back a smile. *It's finally over.*

As they approached the marina Elizabeth could see from the bow of the yacht the flashing blue and red lights of the squad cars and ambulances that waited for them onshore. The huge inflatable parrot floating above Pirate Perry's swayed in the wind, as if it were welcoming them home.

Matt cut the racer's engine and slowly steered the boat toward the dock with the *Halcyon* in tow. Blue-uniformed officers lined up along the wooden planks as backup in case Eric tried to escape. But Elizabeth doubted that could happen—she'd used enough rope to rig the yacht two times over.

Elizabeth stared dreamily at the back of Matt's sun-streaked hair and sighed to herself. He scratched the top of his head and surveyed the scene before him, obviously confused as to what was going on. Elizabeth found it almost poetic how Matt had been boating so peacefully on the water all this time while the nightmare on the yacht seemed to bypass him completely. Matt seemed like the kind of person who sailed through life pretty easily, letting chaos and craziness fall by the wayside. Goodness seemed to automatically come to him, and in return he gladly passed it on to others.

Then again, Elizabeth hardly knew him well

enough to know if her theory was true or not. But she was definitely willing to find out. She breathed in the salty sea air excitedly and wondered what the future held in store.

Matt turned around to throw the bumpers over the side of the boat and seemed startled to see Elizabeth leaning against the railing. "Looks like something big's going on over there," he yelled, pointing to the flashing lights. Now that Matt had slowed down the engine, it was easier to shout back and forth between the yacht and the racer. "I hope it's not too serious."

Elizabeth smiled. "They're waiting for us."

"What do you mean?" he called. The racer bumped up against the side of the dock, and Matt threw out a line to anchor it. When he turned back to Elizabeth, his brow furrowed in confusion and his eyes widened as he apparently noticed the bloodstains on her shirt. "What happened? Are you all right?"

"Everybody's fine," Elizabeth answered, holding her hand out to him as they docked. "Help me down, and I'll tell you the whole story."

They disembarked together, with Jessica and Nick just a few feet behind them. As soon as they were safely on the dock the police rushed the yacht, going after Eric. The paramedics were waiting with two stretchers nearby for Jessica and Nick, and while they were treated for their injuries, Elizabeth pulled Matt aside and told him everything.

"I feel like such a jerk," Matt said when she was done. His blue eyes drooped in the corners. "I'm sorry I didn't help you—I had no idea any of this was happening."

"It's all right, Matt. How could you have known?" Elizabeth looped her arm through his as they strolled along the boardwalk, out of the way of the commotion.

"I hope they lock up that nut for life."

"Me too," Elizabeth replied, her stomach fluttering like a hummingbird's wings as she tried to get up the courage to ask him out. "You were really great, Matt. I don't know what would've happened to Nick and Jessica if it hadn't been for you."

Matt shyly looked down at his feet. "I did what anybody would've done," he said with sincere humility. "I just happened to be the one who was around at the time."

Thank goodness for that, Elizabeth thought.

"Well, you went above and beyond the call of duty," she answered. "I can't think of too many people who would've been kind enough to offer me their radio or take me out on the water during a storm to find my lost sister or to—" Elizabeth cut herself off, suddenly aware that she was gushing. She could feel the heat rushing to her face; she was probably scarlet by now. "What I'm trying to say, Matt, is thanks for all you've done."

"It was my pleasure," Matt answered sweetly as they reached the end of the boardwalk. "If you ever need anything at all, you should look me up."

"You should look me up." Elizabeth turned the words over in her mind as she watched the surf roll onto the beach. *What exactly does he mean by that? Is he saying I should definitely stop by sometime—meaning tomorrow? Or is he just being polite—meaning never?* Elizabeth stood there stiffly in awkward silence, trying to decide what kind of move she should make, if any.

"I sure do love it out here," Matt said suddenly, as if he sensed a need to pick up the lull in the conversation. "It's so beautiful and peaceful."

This is your chance. . . . You have to say something. . . . Be direct. . . . Elizabeth's mouth suddenly went dry. *Ask him now or you'll regret it forever. . . .*

Elizabeth swallowed hard and felt herself chickening out by the second. "So, Matt, what are you going to do now?" she asked, her voice breaking with a squeak on the word *now*.

What a way to be direct, Liz, she berated herself, swearing to be a little more specific this time. "Do you, um, have any plans?"

Matt ran his fingers through his thick, sandy-colored hair and stared out over the water. "I have a lot to do—I'm leaving for a couple of races the day after tomorrow. I'm heading south toward Baja and I won't be back for two months."

There's your answer. Elizabeth's fluttering stomach felt like it had been stung by an angry bee. *Lucky you—you never had to ask the question.* Elizabeth sighed quietly, grateful to have been spared the humiliation. Why was everything that seemed perfect always too good to be true?

"That sounds fabulous," Elizabeth answered casually. "I hope you have a great time."

Matt nodded and lowered his head. "Too bad you can't come along with me. We make a pretty good sailing team."

"We do, don't we?" Elizabeth said with a shy grin, her bruised ego somewhat restored. "Especially when it comes to rescuing sinking ships."

Matt suddenly turned and took both of Elizabeth's hands in his, giving her a smile so warm and wonderful, it could have melted the polar ice caps. "It really *was* a pleasure spending time with you, Elizabeth. I mean it. And I hope everything goes well for your sister and her boyfriend."

Elizabeth's stomach started tingling again. "Thanks—I'll tell them."

"Maybe someday we'll meet on the high seas."

"That would be nice," Elizabeth whispered, bravely masking her disappointment. "I'd like that."

Matt gently pulled Elizabeth toward him and kissed her tenderly on the cheek, his lips warm and comforting against her soft skin. The fresh smell of the ocean breeze, the rush of the tumbling surf, the warm yellow rays of the sun, and the sweet kiss of a gorgeous guy Elizabeth would probably never see again conspired to make the moment a single, perfect memory.

As she watched Matt walk down the long boardwalk back to his boat, Elizabeth smiled into the sun, grateful for the snapshot of romance she would forever keep cherished in her heart.

*   *   *

"Hey, Fox, don't you know how to take a vacation?"

Buttoning up a clean shirt, Nick laughed and

walked away from the ambulance over to where Chief Wallace was standing. "I guess trouble seems to follow me wherever I go, sir."

Chief Wallace thrust a hand out from the sleeve of his trench coat and firmly shook Nick's hand, giving him a congratulatory pat on the back. "Great work, Detective. Sorry I was so hard on you before."

Nick bowed his head, feeling the shameful memories converging on him like vultures on a carcass. "You had every right to be. Considering how the situation turned out with Katherine Horstmueller—"

"Look, Nick." Chief Wallace placed a firm hand on Nick's shoulder as they walked side by side toward the boat launch. "I know you blame yourself for what happened to her, but—"

"It *was* my fault, though," Nick insisted. "Her death was an indirect result of my negligence. I'm willing to take the fall for that."

The chief shook his head adamantly. "First of all, you don't know for sure that Griffin was going to turn her over when he got the ransom. In fact, the odds were against it."

Nick's green eyes narrowed. "What do you mean?"

Chief Wallace pulled a stack of papers from the inside pocket of his coat. "After you called on the radio, we did a little research on Eric

Griffin. For starters, he's got a rap sheet a mile long. But the kicker is, we were able to cross-reference some of the details of the Horstmueller case with five unsolved kidnapping cases, and guess who came up as a very strong possible suspect in each case?"

"Eric Griffin."

"Right you are." The chief smacked the papers against the palm of his hand. "In three out of the five cases, Nick, the victims died while in custody of the kidnapper. *Three out of five.* Griffin is to blame for Katherine Horstmueller's death—not you."

Nick felt the burden release from his shoulders, but not completely. While the odds were in his favor, Nick didn't believe in taking bets when it came to human life. It had been a tragic, costly mistake that he'd made that day, and there was no way of knowing if circumstances would've been any different if Nick had kept his cool. All he knew was that an innocent woman was dead, that he was partly responsible, and that there was nothing Chief Wallace or anyone short of Katherine Horstmueller herself could say that would convince him otherwise.

The paramedics carried a stretcher onto the dock with a barely conscious Eric Griffin strapped onto it. Nick watched as five officers surrounded the wanted man, making sure he didn't escape their custody as he was loaded into the ambulance. Nick supposed he ought to feel some sort of pride or accomplishment from capturing a career criminal who'd made many people suffer, but all he could think about was how sad it was to see another life go to waste.

Nick's heart lifted as he saw Jessica leaving the ambulance. She was smiling again, and her eyes sparkled. "Jessica deserves the credit, Chief," Nick said proudly, wrapping his arms around her. "She did all the work."

Jessica smiled coyly. "And with a great deal of panache, I might add."

Chief Wallace chuckled. "Well, after making a capture like that one, you *both* deserve a vacation—a real one this time, with honors," he said, taking out his checkbook. "Name your destination and I'll take care of it."

"Wow, thanks!" Jessica breathed excitedly.

Nick scratched his chin thoughtfully. "What do you say, Jess? Are you up for another cruise?"

"No way!" Jessica shouted, shoving him playfully. "I never want to go on another cruise for as long as I live. What's the total opposite of sailing?"

"I don't know—something you'd do in the

desert," Chief Wallace said.

"Or the Grand Canyon," Nick added.

"Or maybe just staying close to home," Jessica said. "I think I've had my fill of excitement for a while."

Nick kissed Jessica's forehead tenderly. "I don't care if we stay in Sweet Valley. As long as we're together, it'll be perfect."

"And cheap," Chief Wallace said enthusiastically, tucking his checkbook back into his coat pocket. "My bank account tells me there isn't a better way for you two to spend your vacation."

Jessica was counting the seconds until all the police cars and ambulances left and the commotion finally calmed down so that she and Nick would finally have a few quiet moments to themselves, but no one seemed to be going anywhere. The detectives were collecting evidence from the yacht, a Coast Guard helicopter was being dispatched to rescue the sinking schooner and recover the body of Katherine Horstmueller, and a large crowd of bystanders had gathered around the docks to see what was going on. Not to mention the photographers and journalists who were taking millions of pictures and asking tons of annoying questions. The whole scene made

Jessica's head spin.

While the crowd overtook the *Halcyon* like a team of worker ants, Nick suddenly grabbed Jessica's hand and tugged her away from the mass of people. "What do you say we get out of here for a little while?"

"Lead the way." Jessica sighed with relief and glanced up at the advancing clouds that suddenly covered the afternoon sky. Nick took off, still holding Jessica's hand, and they ran like children through the narrow, cobblestoned streets of the marina. They ran past abandoned warehouses and empty garages, storage facilities and empty parking spaces. Jessica had almost forgotten how good it felt to have solid ground beneath her feet and Nick's warm hand in hers.

"Stop! I can't run anymore!" Jessica panted between breathless giggles. But Nick still dragged her on, pulling her around the corner into a darkened alley where no one was around. There Nick kissed her passionately against the crumbling brick wall, his body pressed against hers, their breath mingling as one. Jessica was consumed by the fire of the moment, unable to remember the horrible past or speculate on the future, knowing only that she had to treasure each second as though it was the most important time of her life.

A light mist of rain began to fall from the

gray sky, covering the cobblestones with little dark dots. Jessica felt the drops falling through her fingers. "I *hate* water." She groaned aloud. "Do you think we'll ever want to take showers again?"

"Or baths, for that matter," Nick added as his lips traced the contours of Jessica's jawline. Jessica started to giggle in spite of herself but stopped short when Nick stared intensely at her, his emerald green eyes penetrating the depths of her soul. "You know I love you, don't you?" Nick said simply.

Jessica wrapped her arms around his neck, marveling at the way the soft rain seemed to catch on the tip of Nick's dark lashes. "Of course. I love you too." She touched the side of his face. "I never doubted that."

Nick looked away, his sensuous lips trembling with emotion. "It's just that I feel so terrible about leaving you on the boat alone. . . . I should never have left you."

Gently she took his palm and placed it over her heart. "Trust me, Nick," Jessica said, feeling the strength of Nick's undying love with every beat. "You didn't."

Win a *Beach* Vacation!

Enter our **Hot Summer Fun** Sweepstakes!

RETURN COMPLETED ENTRY TO:

Hot Summer Fun Sweepstakes
Bantam Doubleday Dell, Series Marketing
1540 Broadway, 20th Floor
New York, NY 10036

_____

_____ State _____ Zip _____

Date of Birth _____ / _____ / _____
                     Month   Day   Year